How far will Rexcor go for victory?

Junker's car spun out of control, careening right into Megan's path.

Megan fired her rocket boosters.

WHHHOOOOSSSHHHH!

Her Unlimited Division super racer blasted into the air, barely clearing Junker's spinning wreck by inches.

Silently observing this action from the pit, Spex pressed a button on his remote control. An unseen microwave beam fired from the front of the device, striking and scrambling the control systems on Megan's racer.

The maneuvering jets on Megan's car started wildly firing at random. The racer tumbled end over end through the air. "Something's wrong!" Megan cried, frantically flipping levers, struggling to regain control of her vehicle. "The guidance systems aren't responding. I've got to eject!"

Megan pulled the lever to release her Rescue Racer—the combination lifeboat and escape pod, which was designed to eject from the car in case of emergency and bring the driver to safety.

Nothing happened.

Again and again Megan yanked on the release lever with the same result. The world whipped by her window in a rotating blur. She was trapped inside a car she had designed, spinning through the air, wildly out of control.

Collect all these awesome NASCAR Racers books!

NASCAR Racers: *How They Work*

NASCAR Racers: *Official Owner's Manual*

NASCAR Racers #1: *The Fast Lane*

AND COMING IN JULY 2000

NASCAR Racers #3: *Tundra 2000*

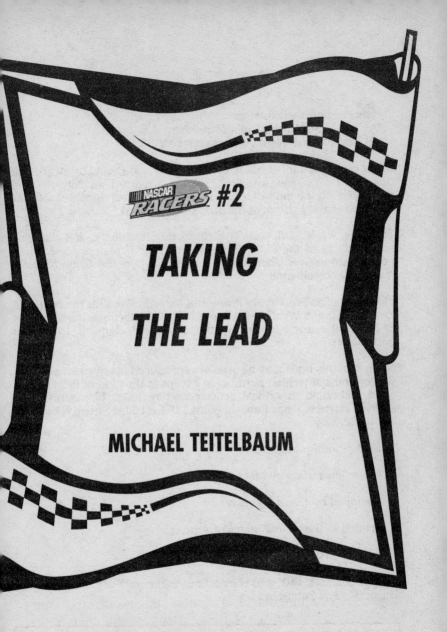

NASCAR RACERS™ #2

TAKING

THE LEAD

MICHAEL TEITELBAUM

HarperEntertainment
An Imprint of HarperCollinsPublishers

HarperEntertainment
An Imprint of HarperCollins*Publishers*
10 East 53rd Street, New York, NY 10022-5299

This is a work of fiction. The characters, incidents, and dialogue are products of the author's imagination, or if real, are used fictitiously. Any resemblance to actual events or persons, living or dead, is entirely coincidental.

First printing: May 2000

Cover illustration by Mel Grant

Designed by Susan Sanguily

Printed in the United States of America

ISBN 0-06-107229-X

Visit HarperEntertainment on the World Wide Web at
www.harpercollins.com

10 9 8 7 6 5 4 3 2 1

1

*R*excor Raceway, home track of Team Rexcor, shook to its foundation as the dozen Unlimited Division cars exploded past the grandstand on another pass. The cars entered a steeply banked turn, practically flipping the drivers upside down as they negotiated the angle. It was a move that would have been impossible for any normal racecar. But these were no normal racecars.

Rrrroooaarrr!

These were the brand-new, high-tech marvels of NASCAR's experimental Unlimited Division, and they were capable of zooming around the track at speeds approaching 400 miles per hour. Behind the wheels of these modern miracles of engineering were no ordinary drivers, either. These steely-nerved hotshots were as precisely equipped for their jobs as the machines they commanded.

Megan Fassler of Team Fastex gripped the wheel of her speeding machine and made her move. Megan, whose Team Fastex nickname was "Spitfire," was not only a highly talented member of the four-driver Fastex team. She was also a brilliant engineer who had designed many of the special features of her team's Unlimited Division racers.

"Come on, out of my way," Megan muttered, as she passed two slower cars and swept through a turn, passing another.

She glanced at the TV monitor and caught a glimpse of her Fastex teammates, Steve "Flyer" Sharp and Carlos "Stunts" Rey in the middle of the pack. They were gaining, too. Megan turned her attention back to what was happening on the track ahead of her. A high-speed battle raged between two cars jockeying for the lead. One car was driven by Megan's fourth Fastex teammate, Mark McCutchen, known to racing fans as "Charger." Charger gunned his engine and slipped inches ahead of Team Rexcor's Hondo Hines, better known as "Specter." Hines was right on Charger's rear bumper now, pushing his vehicle and scraping, metal to metal, against the back of Charger's car.

2

Wham!

Inside his car, Charger was jolted forward against the tight grip of his shoulder restraint. "Back off, Specter!" Charger shouted. "If I wanted to play bumper cars I'd go to the amusement park!"

Spying a sliver of daylight, Hines cut his steering wheel sharply to the left and floored his accelerator. "Move over, loser," he snarled venomously, as his racer shot forward.

Charger reacted instinctively. A third-generation NASCAR driver, racing was in Mark McCutchen's genes. He swiftly angled to his left, eliminating the daylight between his streaking racer and the inside edge of the track, leaving Hines stuck behind his right bumper.

Megan now gained on Hines, taking her cues off his moves, looking for an opening as the three supercars blasted down the track.

"Just give me some daylight, boys," Megan said, tight-lipped, her concentration fierce.

Like a three-car string attached by some invisible chain, the racers jockeyed for an opening, bashing bumpers and scraping fenders.

The three drivers hit a straightaway and Hines made a daring, sudden move. Pulling his steering wheel hard to the right, Hines cut sideways, sliding up toward the high side of the track, trying to pass Charger from above.

Megan spotted the opening she'd been waiting

for. Her eyes widened as she mashed her foot down onto the accelerator, heading for the space vacated by Hines.

Brrrrooommmm!

She flashed alongside Charger.

Charger turned his head and smiled broadly at Megan. "Duck did a great job setting your car up for the race!" he said into the microphone in his helmet.

Megan stayed focused on her driving. She returned a quick nod. "Everything's running right, Charger!" she shouted over the noise of her racecar. "I have a feeling today's my day!"

With that, Megan flipped a switch on her dashboard and her powerful rocket boosters flared to life.

Whhhoooossshhhh!

A flare of red and orange tore from the back of her racer. She exploded past Charger into the lead, her rear end fishtailing as she overtook her teammate.

The Fastex Independently Mobile Pit unit, known as the IMP, sat just off the track. The IMP was a self-contained garage on wheels. Each team in the Unlimited Division had an IMP and a pit crew waiting inside to keep the supercars on the track moving at top efficiency.

Inside the Fastex IMP, Jack Fassler and Duck

Dunaka watched the race intently. Duck Dunaka was Team Fastex's crew chief and head mechanic. Jack Fassler, the owner of Fastex Corporation, was responsible for the creation of the NASCAR Unlimited Division and sponsored Team Fastex. Jack Fassler also happened to be Megan's father.

Jack Fassler frowned momentarily at his daughter's on-screen image. Megan had joined the team as a driver against her father's wishes. He felt that she belonged in the engineering lab, where her razor-sharp mind could be working on ways to perfect Unlimited Division cars. But Megan longed to drive, and she quickly earned her father's respect with her ability behind the wheel.

"She's going all the way, Duck!" Jack shouted. His frown was replaced with a proud grin as he pointed at Megan's car blasting past Charger's.

Duck's forehead crinkled and his lips pursed together as he gave Jack a skeptical look. "I thought you didn't want Megan to drive," he said to his boss.

"I don't," Jack replied, his excited expression turning serious. "But if she's going to drive, I want her to win!"

2

*T*he headquarters building of the Rexcor Corporation was a huge, black, ominous-looking tower. Rexcor was the company that built the cars driven by the Rexcor racing team, Team Fastex's fiercest competitors.

Garner Rexton, owner of Rexcor, watched the race from his luxury suite overlooking Rexcor Raceway. Only Rexton wasn't looking out the huge window that took up one entire wall of the suite and gave a perfect view of the track below. Rather, Garner Rexton sat with his back to the window and its spectacular view and watched his cars compete on a giant-screen television.

He sat alone in the extravagant yet elegant suite like a spider in a high-tech web. Rexton and Jack Fassler had once been best friends and business partners. But the greater their success, the further apart they grew. Then they both fell in love with the same woman. When she chose Jack, Rexton declared himself Fassler's sworn enemy, determined at any cost to destroy Jack Fassler and the company he worked so hard to create.

Rexton leaned back in his plush leather chair and watched Megan burst past Charger on the giant screen before him. He flipped a switch on a communications panel built into the arm of the chair. "Spex," he said softly.

In the pit at Rexcor Raceway, Spex, the Rexcor crew chief, activated the monitor on his cybernetic harness. Spex was a human being, but you'd never know it by looking at him. This Rexcor engineer was covered in a high-tech suit that made him look like a robot. His cybernetic eyes stared straight ahead, like two red chunks of glowing coal, lifeless yet intimidating. His harness contained communications systems, vision enhancements, computer interfaces, built-in tools, retractable wheels, and a video monitor on which Garner Rexton's glaring face now appeared.

"Activate the device," Rexton ordered.

"The prototype has not been fully tested," Spex replied in his cold, mechanical voice.

"Then test it now!" Rexton barked. "I don't intend to lose this race—especially not to Jack Fassler's daughter!"

"Yes, Mr. Rexton," Spex replied. A small panel on Spex's metallic body slid open. Out popped a remote control, which Spex grabbed; then he punched in a series of commands.

The commands from Spex's remote were received by a camera mounted on the Team Rexcor hauler. Each team's hauler served as a high-tech home away from home. It contained a lounge for the drivers and mechanics, living quarters, and state-of-the-art communications equipment. The king-size vehicles were also used to haul the racecars themselves from track to track, giving the large trucks their name.

It was not unusual for a hauler to have a camera mounted on the outside to keep track of a race. However, the piece of equipment on Team Rexcor's hauler, which looked like a camera and now rotated in response to Spex's command, was far from an innocent recording device.

The mysterious "camera" locked in on its target: Megan's car. The image of her car appeared on Spex's monitor, with two targeting crosshairs precisely lining up the vehicle as it sped around the track.

"Target locked," Spex reported, his chilling voice

bleating from a small speaker on the arm of Garner Rexton's chair.

Without a word, Rexton punched a button on his communications panel.

"Junker," he called. "On Spitfire's next pass, let's see how well she handles an emergency!"

Rexton's voice reached the streaking car driven by Team Rexcor's Diesel Spitz, nicknamed "Junker." Junker raced in the United States since being banned from driving in his native Europe, and got his nickname because he loved to wreck cars—both his own and those of other drivers. "I will be blowing my own tire," Junker replied to Rexton in his heavy accent. "That is always much exciting."

"Just make sure it looks like an accident," Rexton ordered.

"Same as always," Junker replied.

Down on the track, Megan roared up right behind Junker. She shifted into high gear, stepped hard on the accelerator, and whipped her steering wheel sharply to the left. As she began to pass him, the usually aggressive Junker seemed to pull his slower car out of the way.

Megan didn't question the move, she just pulled up beside Junker, ready to blow by him. When the two cars were even, Junker yanked on a hidden lever beneath his dashboard.

Bang!

His left rear tire exploded with a deafening boom.

9

Junker's car spun out of control, careening right into Megan's path!

Without pausing to think, Megan fired her rocket boosters.

Whhhooooossshhhh!

Her Unlimited Division super racer blasted into the air, clearing Junker's spinning wreck by inches.

Silently observing this action from the pit, Spex pressed a button on his remote control. The false camera on the Rexcor hauler hummed with power, crackling with electronic noise. An unseen microwave beam fired from the front of the device, striking and scrambling the control systems on Megan's racer.

The maneuvering jets on Megan's car started wildly firing at random, causing her racer to tumble end over end through the air. "Something's wrong!" Megan screamed, frantically flipping levers, struggling to regain control of her vehicle. "The guidance systems aren't responding. I've got to eject!"

Megan pulled the lever to release her Rescue Racer, the escape pod designed to eject from the car in case of emergency and bring the driver to safety.

Nothing happened.

Again and again Megan yanked on the release lever with the same result. The world whipped by her window in a blur. She was trapped inside a car she had designed, spinning through the air, wildly out of control.

3

"Megan's Rescue Racer isn't launching!" Jack Fassler shouted in horror, as he and Duck watched from the pit while the booster jets on Megan's car continued to fire randomly. With each flaming spear of red and orange, the car veered uncontrollably, spinning and bobbing through the air in a terrifying death dance.

Bash!

The car slammed into the track wall. Normally, this would have brought it to a stop. But Megan's car was five feet off the ground, tumbling at a tremendous speed. The car flipped up and over the wall, spinning higher into the air, then crashed into a tall communications tower just beyond the track. The smoking, crumpled racer bounced off the tower and ricocheted back toward the track.

Crrraaaasssshhh!

Megan's demolished car slammed down right onto the center of the track.

Whooooomp!

The communications tower that Megan had hit crashed down all around her.

In the nearby pit, Jack and Duck scrambled to the Team Fastex IMP. Jack leaped into the driver's seat and grabbed the vehicle's controls.

"Wait a minute, Jack!" Duck shouted, as he stepped up onto the IMP. "The cars are still racing on the—!"

It was too late. Jack slammed the IMP's control lever forward and the huge truck took off, tires squealing like a NASCAR racer. Duck grabbed on to a handhold mounted on the outside of the IMP to keep himself from being thrown off.

The cluster of tightly grouped racers swung around a turn on the track and came bearing down on the tangled wreckage of what had once been the tower and Megan's car.

The giant electronic flag board that hung suspended above the starting line flashed a picture of a huge red flag, the traditional NASCAR symbol telling drivers to come an immediate stop.

One by one the drivers hit their emergency rocket brakes, flames shooting from the fronts of their racers, as their tires squealed in protest. Several cars swerved dangerously, skidding across the track.

Carlos "Stunts" Rey, of Team Fastex, headed right for a skidding Rexcor car. In a bold move he usually saved to pass another car during a race, Stunts fired the maneuvering jets on the left side of his racer. The flaming rocket boosters lifted his car up onto its two right wheels, which passed only inches from the top of the out-of-control Rexcor vehicle then stuttered to a halt.

A few seconds later, Steve "Flyer" Sharp, the fourth member of Team Fastex, skidded toward the smoking wreckage. His right foot hit his brakes with all his strength, but he knew that he was quickly running out of track. Flyer swiftly flipped two switches on his dashboard. Wings sprang from each side of his car, then his turbojet boosters fired, lifting the racer into the air and over the twisted mass of his teammate's car. He screeched to a stop just beyond.

Charger reared to a stop nearby. He was out of his car before it had finished sliding, and he ran, full speed, toward the wreck.

"Megan!" he cried. Charger reached Megan's car in seconds. As gently as he could, he pulled her unconscious form from the smoldering heap of

13

twisted metal. He hurried off the track with Megan in his arms just as . . .

Ka-blaaaammm!

Megan's demolished car exploded in a massive fireball of orange and red.

A fire-fighting helicopter swooped down toward the flaming wreckage, spraying fire-retardant foam over the blazing ruin.

Charger kneeled down, carefully placing Megan on the ground while still cradling her limp body, unwilling to let go. "You're going to be all right, Spitfire," he whispered. "You're going to be all right . . . Megan."

Stunts and Flyer ran over and stood next to Charger.

"She's not gonna, gonna—" Stunts sputtered, out of breath and unable to voice the rest of his thought.

"She's tough," Flyer said, though his voice betrayed his concern. "She'll be okay."

The air ambulance helicopter churned up the dust and grit on the track and practically blew the drivers over as it landed next to Charger and Megan. A team of medics dashed from the chopper and lifted Megan onto a gurney.

As the medics wheeled Megan to the waiting helicopter the Team Fastex IMP came braking to a screeching stop. Duck was at the controls now. Jack leaped from the IMP before it had fully stopped and

raced to his daughter's side just as she was loaded into the chopper. Jack scrambled aboard alongside her.

"Come on!" he shouted to be heard over the helicopter's thrashing rotors. "Let's get her to a hospital!"

Charger watched helplessly as the chopper lifted off and then grew ever smaller in the smoke-filled sky.

4

Beep-beep-beep-beep . . .

The heart monitor in Megan's hospital room piped softly and steadily. Megan, her head bandaged, lay unconscious in her bed. Charger sat beside her, talking, hoping she could hear him.

"You have to fight your way back, Megan," Charger said, mustering all the enthusiasm he could. "You can beat this thing if you just keep fighting."

He leaned in close to Megan's ear. "The team's counting on you," he whispered. Then, looking around to make sure they were alone, he added, "*I'm* counting on you. I don't know what I'd do if—"

The door to Megan's room burst open, cutting off Charger's thought. Jack Fassler and his wife, Libby, rushed into the room. Although they had once been very much in love, over time they grew apart and eventually went their separate ways. They disagreed about many things, but the one thing they still had in common was their extraordinary love for their daughter.

"The doctor says she's stable," Jack reported to Libby, not realizing that Charger was in the room. "But they won't know more until she regains consciousness."

Jack and Libby spotted Charger and stopped short.

"I—I just," Charger stammered, embarrassed to be found in Megan's room. "Well, the doctor said it was all right to come in." He smiled awkwardly at the Fasslers and left the room.

Jack moved close to Megan's side.

"I never should have let her drive," Jack berated himself, staring down at his motionless daughter.

Libby stepped up beside him. "There's no way we could have stopped her, Jack," she offered. "Megan makes her own choices. In everything."

Duck Dunaka stepped into the room. "Jack," he began. "Sorry to interrupt, but I need to talk to you. Alone."

"Not now, Duck," Jack snapped, annoyed at the interruption. "We'll talk later."

Duck stared at his boss. "It can't wait, Jack," he said tersely.

Jack hurried from the room followed closely by Duck. In the hallway, Duck held up the damaged remains of a metal box. A charred computer motherboard could clearly be seen through a tear in the box.

"This is the on-board computer from Megan's car," Duck explained.

"Is *this* what you brought me out here to show me?" Jack asked impatiently. "This is what couldn't wait?!"

"The circuits have been scrambled, Jack," Duck said. Then, looking his boss in the eye, he added, "And, it happened *before* the crash!"

Jack glared at Duck. "You're the crew chief!" he exploded. "You're supposed to double-check those circuits before every race!"

"You don't have to tell me my job!" Duck shot back defensively.

"If you'd *done* your job, maybe my daughter wouldn't be lying in there in a coma!" Jack shouted, pointing to Megan's room. He spun on his heel and stormed away.

Duck's head dropped to his chest dejectedly. He looked down at the crumpled box in his hands, then looked up at Jack. "You have to talk to me, Jack!" he called after his boss. "I can't handle this alone!"

Jack ignored him and kept walking.

"Jack!" Duck shouted, his strained voice echoing down the hospital hallway.

Outside the hospital a television crew arrived and set up. A Team Fastex driver was lying inside in a coma, and that was big news. Add to that the fact that the driver just happened to be the daughter of the owner of Fastex Corporation. That was *really* big news.

Anchorwoman Pat Anther faced the TV camera, microphone in hand, and began her remote broadcast. "Driver Megan Fassler is in a coma after a terrifying crash at the Rexcor Raceway this afternoon."

Suddenly, behind Pat Anther, Duck stormed out the hospital's main entrance followed closely by Jack. Both men were furious.

"I don't want to hear any more excuses, Dunaka!" Jack barked at his crew chief. "Those cars are *your* responsibility!"

"Not anymore!" Duck declared. "I won't work for someone who doesn't trust me!"

Pat Anther's mouth dropped open—an argument was happening between the head of Fastex and his crew chief right before her eyes! This was a very juicy bit of news—and she just happened to be here with her crew! "Get this on camera!" she ordered the camera operator, who quickly zoomed in on Jack and Duck.

"I'm gonna show you just how much Team Fastex needs me!" Duck shouted.

That night in the communications room of the Rexcor Team hauler, Garner Rexton watched this very scene unfolding. As the image of Jack and Duck arguing flashed on his TV monitor, a sinister smile spread across Rexton's face.

"I quit!" Duck shouted on the TV screen. He stormed off, and his image was replaced by a close-up shot of Pat Anther.

"And there you have it," the newscaster reported. "The tragic aftermath of a tragic accident. Team Fastex crew chief Douglas "Duck" Dunaka has resigned. Could this knock Team Fastex out of the hunt for the NASCAR Unlimited Division Championship? Stay tuned!"

The evil grin on Rexton's face grew wider as he watched. Then he sighed in satisfaction.

As the broadcast ended, in the garage area of Rexcor Raceway, Duck Dunaka was loading his tools into his battery-powered rolling toolbox on wheels. He was preparing to leave Team Fastex.

Charger, Stunts, and Flyer strolled into the garage and saw Dunaka packing his belongings.

"I guess it's true then," Charger said with a frown. "You've quit Team Fastex."

Duck tossed the last of his tools into the toolbox then turned to the drivers. "It's true enough," he replied flatly.

Charger looked right at Duck. "You're part of Team Fastex, Duck!"

"Yeah," Stunts agreed. "The part that keeps the cars running!"

"You can't quit," Flyer added. "We need you."

"I'm quitting for the good of the team," Duck explained. "Someday you'll understand." Then he pressed a button on a remote control, and his tool-box rolled out of the Team Fastex section of the garage, heading for the Team Rexcor area.

In the Team Rexcor section of the garage, Spex's mechanical body was bent over the engine of Lyle Owens's car. Owens was a Team Rexcor driver who had driven for Team Fastex until Jack Fassler learned why his nickname was "The Collector," and fired him. Owens liked to collect the smashed-up pieces of his competitors' cars.

Spex was fine-tuning Owens's engine when Duck Dunaka's rolling toolbox bumped into Rexcor's robotic crew chief.

"What?" Spex cried, lifting his metallic head from under the hood and whirling around to face Duck, who stared up defiantly at Spex's eerie robot eyes.

"Your boss around?" Duck asked casually.

Spex stepped menacingly toward Duck, but the ex–Fastex crew chief stood his ground. A loud *beeeep* froze Spex in midstep, as if someone had simply turned him off like a mechanical toy. The video monitor on Spex's midsection flared to life, and the image of Garner Rexton filled the screen.

"What do you want, Dunaka?" Rexton demanded, his voice blaring from a speaker on Spex's chest.

Duck spoke directly to the image on the monitor. "You may have heard," he said offhandedly, "I've left Team Fastex. I'm looking for a job."

Rexton's image glared at Duck. "Why would you want to work for a team that's racing against Fastex?" he asked with suspicion.

Duck leaned in close to the monitor. "Maybe I want to show Jack Fassler just how much he needs me," Duck replied, his voice filled with bitterness.

Rexton paused and thought for a moment. "Revenge is a very powerful motive," he began, quickly adding, "so I've heard. Very well, Dunaka. You're my new head mechanic—working under Spex."

Duck backed away from the monitor. "I'll be here first thing in the morning, Mr. Rexton," he replied. Then he turned and strode away.

Lyle Owens, who wanted revenge against Jack Fassler and Team Fastex almost as much as Garner

Rexton did, walked around to face the monitor on Spex.

"You'd better keep an eye on him, Mr. Rexton," Owens suggested.

"I keep my eye on everyone," Rexton replied. Then his image on the monitor disappeared as the screen on Spex's chest went dark.

Owens scratched his head, feeling uncomfortable for some reason. Then he glanced over his shoulder and spied a huge video monitor containing a large image of Garner Rexton staring down at him. He shuddered, then turned back to his car.

5

Back in Megan's hospital room, Jack and Libby Fassler sat by the head of their daughter's bed. They glanced sadly at Megan— still bandaged, still unconscious—then looked at each other. There seemed to be nothing left to say and nothing they could do.

And then Megan's eyes fluttered open for the first time since the crash. "Mom. Dad," she said weakly. "The race. Who won?"

Libby smiled broadly, relief washing over her whole body. "Now I *know* she's going to be all right!" she said.

Jack placed his hand on Megan's and gave it a gentle squeeze. "The track was blocked by the crash," he explained. "They had to cancel. They'll restart the race this weekend."

Megan tried to get up. "I've got to get my car rebuilt!" she exclaimed. Then she groaned and sank back into the bed. It was a toss-up as to which part of her body hurt the most.

Jack looked down at her sternly. "You're not getting out of that bed until the doctors say you're well, young lady," he reprimanded in his most fatherly voice.

A look of concern now mixed with the look of pain on Megan's face. "You're not going to try to keep me from racing again, are you?" she asked.

Jack glanced over at Libby, then looked down at Megan and smiled. "Your car will be ready when you are . . . Spitfire!" he reassured her.

Megan closed her eyes and drifted off to sleep.

The next morning, the garage area of Rexcor Raceway was buzzing with activity. Pit crews from all the racing teams were hard at work, fixing, preparing, and fine-tuning their cars for the upcoming rerunning of the race that had ended so horribly for Megan.

In the Team Fastex section of the garage, Charger, Stunts, and Flyer lined up in front of Jack Fassler.

The Fastex owner addressed the three other drivers on his team. "Until further notice," he began formally, "I'm taking over as Team Fastex crew chief. I'm new to the job, so I'm asking all of you for your help."

Miles McCutchen, Charger's ten-year-old brother, squeezed between Charger and Stunts. He stepped in front of the drivers and stood straight up at attention, a wrench in one hand, a tire gauge in the other. "You've got it, Mr. Fassler!" Miles said proudly. "I'm ready to give you all the help you need."

Jack's expression changed to one of shock. This was not what he expected. Miles was known more for taking things apart than for putting them back together. Then again, Jack needed all the help he could get.

Jack shrugged his shoulders and nodded. Then he put Miles to work.

Miles tried to be helpful, although his skills as a high-tech NASCAR mechanic did leave plenty of room for improvement. Jack alternately ended up with a face full of oil, a mouth full of black smoke, and a car that left the pit without its rear wheels. Miles smiled sheepishly after each blunder, but Jack just chalked them up to rookie mistakes.

Duck Dunaka watched all this from the nearby Team Rexcor area, shaking his head at the goings-on at Team Fastex, while working with Spex on

Rexcor's cars. When he thought that no one was looking, Duck shuffled over to the Rexcor hauler, then looking back over his shoulder, silently slipped inside.

The inside of the Team Rexcor hauler looked just like every other hauler Duck had ever seen. Spare parts, tools, and tires sat neatly in storage racks. Duck stepped through a door and into the hauler's communications room. This, too, looked pretty normal. Radio-transmitters and receivers, television monitors, and videodisc player-recorders lined the room.

"Let's see," Duck mumbled to himself. "One, two, three, four videodisc recorders. That makes sense. Four cars to a team, four cameras mounted on the team's hauler, one to record each car. And one recorder for each camera." He picked up a stack of discs from a shelf next to the recorders. "That's odd. There are four disc recorders but only three discs. So what happened to the fourth disc?" He stared at the discs and pondered this mystery.

He was so deep in thought that he didn't hear Spex enter the room. Duck yelped in surprise as powerful mechanical arms grabbed him from behind.

"What are you doing here!" Spex demanded, tightening his vicelike grip.

Duck struggled hard to free himself from Spex's

mighty arms. Grunting and groaning and gasping for breath, he finally freed one hand. He reached into his tool belt and pulled out a socket wrench. Straining to the point of almost pulling his shoulder out if its socket, Duck reached around behind Spex and latched on to a motor control bolt, nabbing it with the wrench. Duck's shoulder throbbed with pain as he turned the bolt, again and again, until finally Spex's arms released him and shot straight up into the air.

"What did you do to me?" Spex raged. "Get my arms down!"

"Sure, Spex, old buddy," Duck replied, flexing his own arm before resetting Spex's. "Sorry about that, but you scared me sneaking up like that."

"You are not authorized for hauler entry," Spex stated in his mechanical voice.

Duck held up the three video discs. "I just wanted to check the videos of the last race," Duck explained. "You know, see how the camera setup was working. But I could only find three discs."

Spex roughly grabbed the discs from Duck's hand. "There is no fourth disc," Spex stated flatly. "One of the cameras malfunctioned."

"You want me to take a look at it?" Duck volunteered, as he stepped from the hauler. "I'm pretty good with cameras."

"That won't be necessary," Spex explained, set-

tling into the hauler's cab next to the driver. "The broken camera is being taken for repairs." Just before he slammed the cab door he leaned out and looked right at Duck. "You were hired to work on cars, not cameras," Spex snarled. Then he slammed the door and the hauler sped away.

Duck stared after it, shaking his head and rubbing his sore shoulder.

6

Soft *moonlight cast eerie shad-*
ows on the Brand Rex Research Facility. Owned by
Rexcor, the large stone bunker of a building was
located a few miles from Rexcor Raceway. The steel-
gated doors and high-tech security locks aimed to
send a clear message to visitors: KEEP OUT!

Which was exactly the opposite intention of the
two men who silently crept up to the research facility's loading dock. Their faces covered with ski
masks, the two intruders crouched by the heavy,
reinforced steel loading-dock door.

One of the men pulled a small voltmeter from his

tool belt, which he speedily attached to an electronic keypad lock using alligator clips.

"Mrrumph dtfurt sgtib ti," mumbled the second man.

"Frwipt ya vrpl?" the first man mumbled back. Then, with a frustrated pull, he yanked off the ski mask—revealing the face of Duck Dunaka. "Do we have to wear these things?" he asked his partner. "I can't understand a word that you're saying!"

The other man removed his mask. It was Jack Fassler. "I said it was a great plan you had," Jack whispered, "pretending to quit so you could go to work for Rexcor."

Duck had followed the Rexcor hauler to this building, then contacted Jack. The two returned by darkness of night in a Team Fastex high-tech tow truck.

Duck pulled a pair of needlenose pliers from his tool belt and went to work picking the door's electronic lock. "Well, we haven't proved they sabotaged Megan's car yet," Duck pointed out as he worked.

"I've got a feeling the proof we need is right behind this door," Jack said hopefully.

Click! Whhirrrrr!

The lock disengaged, and the hefty metal door rolled open.

"We're in," Duck announced, returning the tools to his belt. "Let's go."

Duck and Jack slipped into the loading dock, mov-

ing swiftly but silently, keeping their backs pressed against a wall. They stopped at a pile of boxes covered by a canvas tarp.

"Let's see what Spex has been up to," Jack whispered. Then he whipped the canvas off the mountain of boxes.

"Microwave ovens?" Jack said in shock, staring at box after box of conventional microwave ovens, the type anyone might have at home.

Duck opened one of the boxes and, sure enough, inside sat a microwave oven.

"Maybe Spex likes to cook," Duck suggested, shrugging his shoulders. "But why bring a camera to a microwave factory for repair?"

"Let's go find out," Jack said.

The two spies crept deeper into the research facility. They soon came to a huge, hangar-size lab and squatted behind a large crate. In the center of the lab sat the Rexcor hauler. It appeared that one of the hauler's cameras was resting on a large platform. The device lay open, exposing a tangle of wires, computer motherboards, and a small microwave dish that pointed out the camera lens.

Two technicians held the camera in position while Spex ran a scanner from his bodysuit over the open unit. "With these adjustments," Spex began, "the electronic disruption caused by the microwave beam will look more like a natural short circuit."

Crouched in their hiding position, Jack grabbed

Duck's arm. "That's it," he whispered, trying to contain his excitement and his anger. "That must be how they fried the electronics in Megan's car—a concentrated burst of microwaves! And it sounds like they're planning to use it again at tomorrow's race. We've got to stop them before another driver gets hurt . . . or worse!"

Spex looked up suddenly as if he'd heard a noise. He scanned the lab quickly with his computer-enhanced eyes.

Jack nudged Duck and pointed to the open door of a storage vault. Duck nodded and followed Jack into the vault, closing the door behind them as quietly as possible.

Whhirrrrr! Click!

The two men turned and stared at each other. Jack grabbed the door handle and gave it a yank. The door didn't budge. "We're locked in!" Jack said, panic in his voice.

Duck calmly pulled tools from his tool belt, eyeing the complex electronic lock. "Don't have a blowout," Duck counseled. "I'll have that door open in no time."

The following morning, in the pit at Rexcor Raceway, Charger, Flyer, and Stunts paced nervously beside their cars.

"Where's Jack?" Stunts asked excitedly. "We can't run a race without a crew chief!"

"Oh, this is great," Charger muttered. "First Duck quits, and now we lose Jack."

"Yeah," Flyer moaned. "And the race is going to start any second."

A commanding voice boomed over the raceway's loudspeakers. "All drivers to their cars."

Flyer let out a deep sigh, then pulled his helmet over his head. "Come on," he said to the others. "Crew chief or not, we've got a race to run."

The three Team Fastex drivers scrambled into their racers and pressed their start buttons.

Frrroooommm! Frrroooommm! Frrroooommm!

The powerful jet engines of the NASCAR Unlimited Division racers flared to life. Then Charger, Flyer, and Stunts drove off toward the starting line.

A short distance away, the Rexcor hauler, with Spex at the wheel, pulled into the Rexcor pit area. It was returning to the track from its all-night microwave mission at the Brand Rex research facility. Spex jumped from the hauler's cab and started setting up its four cameras—including the one containing the deadly microwave beam!

7

*T*he mood in Megan's hospital room was much cheerier than it had been a few days earlier. Megan was well on her way to making a full recovery. At that moment she was sitting up in bed watching TV.

Libby came into the room and smiled at her daughter. "Has the race started yet?" she asked.

"Come on, Fastex!" Megan shouted at the TV screen. "Let's kick some bumper!"

Libby chuckled. "I guess that answers my question," she said to herself softly.

• • •

Vrrooomm! Vrrooomm! Vrrooomm!

One by one the supercars of NASCAR's Unlimited Division sizzled down the track at Rexcor Raceway. The makeup race was under way, and Team Fastex was out picking up where they had left off when Megan had her terrible crash. And so was Team Rexcor.

Flyer and Lyle Owens swept through a steep banked turn, engines roaring. At the peak of the turn their cars were almost upside down, but their tires gripped the road like a jungle cat's claws. The drivers maneuvered confidently through the turn.

Flyer shifted gears as he returned to the straightaway. Lyle Owens, The Collector, was right behind him.

Owens reached for a lever under his dashboard. "Join the collection, Flyer," he snarled, as he yanked on the lever and fired his rocket boosters.

Owens shot forward, five feet off the ground, leaping right at Flyer.

Flyer caught sight of this move and reacted swiftly. "It's flying time!" he announced as he flipped two switches. Instantly, wings sprang from either side of his racer and his turbojets fired in a gush of orange flame. His racer shot into the air.

Which is exactly when Owens landed, hard, right in the spot where Flyer had been. The heavy-footed landing sent a jolt through Owens's body. More important, it sent his racer spinning out of control.

Squeeeaall!

Tires screeched and brakes shrieked as a car driven by a member of another Unlimited Division team plowed right into Owens's spinning vehicle. The two racers went careening off the track in a sliding, tumbling mess.

Flyer retracted his wings and returned his car to the track. "See ya later, Collector," he smirked as he shot into the next turn.

The night had passed excruciatingly slowly for Jack Fassler and Duck Dunaka. Morning had come, the race had begun, and they were still locked inside the storage vault at the Brand Rex Research facility. Their night had been filled with no food, no sleep, and no escape.

"Come on, baby," Duck muttered, as he worked on the lock with a small Allen wrench. Tools of all sizes and shapes were stuck to the door with duct tape—a makeshift workshop for a frustrated mechanic. "I know you're gonna open for me this time."

"You've been saying that for hours, Duck!" Jack growled, as he leaned over Duck's shoulder. Jack glanced at his watch for about the ten thousandth time. "Hurry up! The race has already started by now!"

Duck wheeled around and glared at his boss. "I don't do this for a living, you know!" he shouted.

37

"I'm a mechanic! I work on cars! Next time you get yourself locked inside a vault, try doing it with a locksmith!" Then he shoved a thin, toothpicklike metal tool into a small opening next to the lock's keypad.

Whiirrrr! Click!

Jack and Duck looked at each other. Then they both turned to the door. Duck popped the handle. The door swung open. "I told you I got it this time," Duck said.

They stepped from the storage vault—and found themselves face-to-face with a technician holding a strange-looking microwave contraption. "Hey, you don't work here," the technician observed. He put down the device and pressed a button on the wall.

Jack and Duck turned and dashed through a door leading out of the lab as a piercing alarm flooded the building with sound.

"This way!" Jack shouted, turning down a long hallway—and running right into a security guard.

"Stop!" the guard ordered.

"Okay," Jack said, grabbing Duck's arm and spinning him around. "Maybe that *wasn't* the best way. Run!"

They raced back down the hallway, with the guard giving chase, and made a sharp right turn. "Here!" Jack called, pointing to a door labeled STAIRS. He yanked open the door, and he and Duck rushed through—

38

—only to find themselves outside, on the flat roof of the building. They ran to the edge of the roof, which was surrounded by a metal railing. Peering over the railing, looking straight down, both men realized that it was a long, long way to the ground below.

"There they are!" came a shout from behind them. Jack and Duck pivoted and saw four security guards charging through the stairway door and out onto the roof.

Duck looked at his boss. "Maybe this wasn't such a great plan either!" Jack admitted.

"We're not on our last lap yet!" Duck announced, pulling a roll of duct tape—which he called "duck" tape, and from which he got his nickname—out of his trusty tool belt. He quickly stuck the end of the tape onto the railing, then spooled the tape around the railing, two, three, four times.

Tugging on the tape, he trusted that it would hold them. It would have to. They had nowhere else to go.

"Come on, Jack!" Duck shouted, stepping over the railing and grasping the roll of tape. He jumped off the edge of the roof, rappelling down the side of the building with the roll of tape unspooling as he went.

Duck's feet hit the ground. He released the tape and dashed toward the trees where they had hidden the Fastex tow truck.

Back on the roof, Jack grabbed the tape and

jumped over the side of the roof just as the guards reached him.

They lunged.

And Jack dropped down the side of the building, clutching his sticky gray lifeline.

When he was most of the way down the building, Jack stopped. "Hey!" he called out. "I'm stuck!" His hands were hopelessly tangled in a sticky wad of mangled tape. He tugged hard to free his hands—and the tape broke.

"Yaaaaa!" Jack yelped as he fell the rest of the way to the ground. He landed with a dull thud—just as Duck pulled up in the tow truck, tires squealing.

"You're not supposed to hold it by the sticky side, Jack," Duck reprimanded, leaning out the window of the truck. "Come on. The race has already started."

Dazed and bruised, not to mention covered with a tangled web of silver tape, Jack scrambled into the truck.

"Buckle up," Duck ordered, as he put the truck in gear. "We're burning rubber!" Then he floored the truck.

The speeding truck blasted through a security fence and bounced out onto the road. A few seconds later four Rexcor security cars sped from an underground garage, sirens blaring, tires screaming, chasing after the zooming Fastex tow truck.

8

V*rrooomm! Vrrooomm! Vrrooomm!*

Back at Rexcor Raceway, the pace of the competition shifted into high gear. As the cars zoomed faster, the drivers became more protective of the little section of the track they happened to own for a split second. The massive jet-powered engines of the Unlimited Division racers weren't the only things growing hotter by the second. Tempers burned white hot as well.

And no one raced with more fury than the Rexcor driver known as Junker. Junker came into a turn, side by side with another team's driver. He pulled hard on his steering wheel, slamming into the other car, sending it spinning out of control.

"The track is belonging only to the strong," he declared, glancing back over his shoulder at the smoldering remains of the car he had hit.

Junker returned his view to the track in front of him, only to be greeted by the sight of Flyer's car soaring past his windshield, coming in for a landing, right in front of him!

"Stupid Flyer!" he snarled helplessly. All he could do was watch as Flyer's turbo-boosted racer hit the track and sped off, passing Junker as if he was standing still.

As it was during every NASCAR race, the pit area was a noisy, frantic blur of activity. Cars pulled in. Tires were changed, gas was pumped, repairs were made. Cars pulled out.

In the Rexcor IMP, Spex punched a command into the remote controller he grasped in his metal hand. A short distance away the camera containing the microwave device that had fried the circuits on Megan's racer swiveled in response. The camera pivoted until it found its target: Flyer's car.

Flyer had once again taken to the air, wings deployed, turbo boosters blasting.

Spex locked the image of Flyer's car in the

42

crosshairs on his monitor, then fired. The whining microwave beam streaked from the camera and found Flyer's engine.

Sparks flew from the front of Flyer's racer, which now shook uncontrollably. The wings retracted on their own and the car slammed back to the track, trailing sparks and flames. Flyer tried to regain control, but it was no use. He was battling an enemy he couldn't see, and that he didn't know existed.

He didn't even have time to cry out as his car slammed into the wall.

The Team Fastex tow truck tore down the road. Duck's hands gripped the wheel tightly as his foot jammed down hard on the accelerator.

Jack stuck his head out the passenger window and looked back. "Those Rexcor security guys are gaining on us!" he cried.

"Not to worry," Duck replied calmly. "This thing's got a *big* motor." He shifted gears, mashed the accelerator to the floor, and pulled away from his pursuers.

The tow truck reached a fork in the road. With the skill and precision of a NASCAR driver, Duck pulled the steering wheel hard to the right and zoomed down the right-hand branch of the Y-shaped fork.

Jack kept an eye on the vehicles behind them in

the truck's rearview mirror. He saw two security cars choose the left-hand branch, and two follow them to the right.

"That cuts the odds in half," Jack shouted, smiling for the first time all day.

Duck now had one hand on the steering wheel while the other frantically fiddled with the truck's radio. "Keep it down, will, ya?" he demanded. "I'm trying to find the race."

Static sputtered and crackled, then Duck tuned in the play-by-play, "Problems continue for Team Fastex," the announcer reported. "With one of their three cars already out of the race, and Rexcor holding on to first and second place."

Duck returned both hands to the wheel and stepped a little harder on the gas.

"First and second!" Jack bellowed, turning to Duck. "Couldn't you have done something to *their* cars while you were working for Rexcor?"

"Hey," Duck snapped back, looking his boss right in the eye. "I'm a professional. I don't do sloppy work. No matter who I'm working for."

The two men turned their gaze back to the road and were greeted by a disturbing sight. Just ahead, two Rexcor security cars were parked sideways, completely across the road.

"They've blocked the road!" Jack cried.

"Hang on!" Duck shouted back. Then, without

slowing down a bit, he hauled on the steering wheel.

The truck left the road and climbed up a dirt embankment, leaving the Rexcor guards stunned. Duck powered up the steep rise, then left the ground altogether at the top of the embankment.

The Rexcor guards who were giving chase slammed on their brakes and skidded to a screeching stop just inches from their partners' cars.

Whomp!

The tow truck landed in a large field, bouncing and shaking, but holding together. It sped across the bumpy field, its tires kicking up dirt.

Back at the track, Charger pulled up behind the Rexcor driver named Zorina. Zorina was a driver, model, musician, bodybuilder, and thrill seeker. She drove NASCAR for the kicks, and she didn't care who she hurt. Which made her a perfect Team Rexcor member.

Charger pulled up beside her and started to pass.

"It's not polite to pass a lady," Zorina hissed. Then she swerved right at Charger's car, trying to force him into the wall.

But Charger was ready. He fired his emergency rocket brakes. His racer slowed down in a split second, and Zorina skidded past him, smashing into

the wall instead. Her mangled car bounced off the wall and sputtered to a stop.

"But you're no lady!" Charger said softly, as he brought his car back up to speed.

Suddenly sparks flew from Charger's hood. His rocket boosters and emergency brake rockets fired alternately, pitching the car forward, then jerking it back. Charger slammed forward to the full extent of his shoulder harness, then bashed back into the seat. Brakes fired again, then boosters, and Charger was slammed forward, then back. Charger pulled off the track, cut his engines and glided to a stop on the infield. He was done for the day.

From his luxury suite atop Rexcor Raceway, Garner Rexton watched Charger's car leave the race. He grinned wickedly. Once again his micro-wave beam had destroyed the complex workings of a Team Fastex supercar. He stared down at the image of Spex's face on the monitor before him.

"Two down and one to go," Rexton cackled. "Knock out the last Fastex car, and the race is mine!"

Spex nodded, then lifted his remote control.

9

Stunts was all Team Fastex had left. He was their only driver now, and he knew it. Bobbing and weaving, and using every trick he knew, he scooted pass all the other cars on the track—all but two.

Junker and Specter were battling for the lead. Stunts pulled up behind them, looking for an opening to pass.

In the Rexcor IMP, Spex lined up the microwave camera, its crosshairs now squarely focused on Stunts. Spex's mechanical finger moved toward the firing button, and the end of Team Fastex.

The Fastex tow truck blasted through the infield tunnel of Rexcor Raceway, heading straight for the hauler parking area.

"Hang on to your chrome," Duck shouted, as he released the truck's towing hook. Thick cable unspooled from the back of the truck. Then the sturdy metal hook at the end of the cable snagged the rear bumper of the Rexcor hauler. The cable pulled taut, spinning the hauler sideways and moving the microwave device—

—just as Spex pressed the firing button on his remote.

The crosshairs on Spex's monitor now lined up perfectly—only not on Stunts's car, but on Specter's. A shrill whine sang from the fake camera as the beam shot through the lens.

Specter's engine burst into flames and his car spun out control. He slammed right into Junker. The two Rexcor drivers spun madly down the track, side by side.

"Give me some road!" Stunts shouted, as he approached the two whirling wrecks. "Time for my favorite stunt!" He fired the turbo booster jets on the right side of his car. The racer lifted up onto its two left tires.

Balanced on two wheels, Stunts squeezed past Junker and Specter, threading the needle between

the two out-of-control racers. He shot past the Rexcor cars and crossed the finish line first—still on two wheels!

The crowd went wild. Team Fastex had won the race!

Stunts returned his car to all four wheels, then coasted to an easy stop. A crowd gathered around the winner, who waved to his fans.

Jack and Duck watched from the pit.

"Now that we know what Rexcor was up to, we can adjust our on-board computers," Jack explained.

Duck nodded. "They won't be able to use that microwave beam against us again."

"Us?" Charger asked, as he and Flyer trotted over and joined Jack and Duck. "Does this mean that Duck's part of our team again?"

"You better believe it!" Duck replied. "A team's like a car. Only as good as its parts."

Stunts joined his teammates, who hoisted him up victoriously onto their shoulders.

Jack smiled a bittersweet smile. *The only thing that could have made this better*, he thought, *was if Megan could be here to share this moment.*

The cheering of the crowd poured from the small speaker on the TV and filled Megan's hospital room with sound. Megan watched the screen, propped up

in her bed by a bunch of pillows. Her mother sat in a chair beside her.

"I'm happy for Stunts and the team," Megan said in a voice tinged with sadness. "But I can't help wishing that was me up there on Victory Lane."

"Your time will come," Libby assured her. "Besides, you don't have anything to prove."

Megan swung her legs over the side of the bed. Grimacing with pain, she stood up. "Only to myself," she said, sighing. "Only to myself."

50

10

*F*rrooooommmmm! Frrooooommmmm! Frrooooommmm!

A few days after their victory at Rexcor Raceway, the drivers of Team Fastex whizzed down their home track, Big River Raceway. Jack Fassler had built the raceway as part of New Motor City, what the Fastex Corporation hoped would someday be the automotive and racing capital of the world. Big River Raceway—with a track that ran throughout the city, over the tops of buildings and down through underground autoways—was the crown jewel of Jack Fassler's dream. It was the racetrack of the future, here and now.

Flyer, Charger, and Stunts jockeyed side to side, using every trick they knew to capture the lead. This may have only been a practice run, but to drivers with the competitive spirit of these three, it made no difference—winning was winning.

"Come on, Charger!" Flyer shouted, as he whipped his steering wheel right, then left, trying to carve out an opening and pass his teammate. "Move it or lose it!"

"Lose *you*, you mean!" Charger shot back, shifting into a higher gear, his engine roaring.

Flyer accelerated and pulled even with Charger. Stunts was right behind.

The three cars entered a steep banked turn.

"One against two," Stunts called out. "My kind of odds!"

Stunts dropped down to the low side of the banked turn and pulled even with the others.

"Hey, Stunts!" Charger shouted. "Here's a move I've seen The Collector use!"

Charger slid down the track, clipping Stunts's front fender with the side of his car. Stunts went spinning out of control.

"Can you handle it?" Charger teased.

Stunts pulled hard on his steering wheel, struggling to regain control of his racer. "Handle *this*, Charger!" he snarled.

With one deft maneuver, Stunts pulled out of his spin and popped up onto his two left wheels. "Let's get this show on the road!" he shouted as he punched his rocket boosters. Orange and red flames shot from the rear of his car, sending Stunts roaring between Flyer and Charger, up on two wheels, and into the lead.

Fwam!

Stunts's two left wheels slammed back to the track. He smiled. "I like the view from the front of the pack!" he said with a laugh, enjoying his lead over the others.

Then, impossibly, something swooped out of the sky, heading right for the three cars.

"Enemy aircraft at twelve o'clock!" Flyer announced instinctively, his experience as an Air Force fighter pilot taking over, his hands moving to grasp weapons controls that weren't there.

Then he remembered where he was, and that this just couldn't be happening. "Wait a minute," he said. "What's going on? Why would a fighter plane attack a racetrack?"

The huge flying vehicle lowered, covering an enormous section of the raceway in shadow, and revealing its full form.

"Fighter plane nothing!" Charger shouted, getting a good look. "That's a spaceship!"

The ship was shaped like a gigantic bullet, smooth and sleek, with a rounded tip. Tiny points of brilliant

light flashed up and down its silvery length. The spaceship pivoted in midair—and opened fire! Laser blasts streaked from the ship, bombarding the track.

Charger swerved to avoid a blast and spun off the track. The ship stayed on its target, then vaporized his car with a pinpoint laser shot.

Stunts popped up onto two wheels again. This time not to pass a racer, but to avoid being fried by the alien invader.

Flyer extended his car's wings, fired his turbojets, and took to the air. The spaceship, moving impossibly fast, headed right at Flyer.

"Look out!" he shouted, bracing for a midair crash.

Then Flyer's car and the alien spaceship both froze, hanging in space, the noses of the two airborne vehicles only inches apart!

Big River Raceway, the alien ship, and in fact, the whole background began to dissolve, breaking up into computer static, then vanishing.

The drivers were actually in the simulation room inside the headquarters of Fastex Corporation, training on Virtual Reality simulators. Each driver sat in a racing simulator cockpit pod, wearing a VR helmet. The cockpit was designed to look like the inside of a real NASCAR Unlimited Division racer. It tilted and shook to give the simulation a realistic feel, while the images of the track and the other cars

flashed inside the VR helmets, making the drivers feel as if they were really racing.

Jack and Megan Fassler sat at the controls of the simulator. Megan still wore some bandages and had a little trouble walking, but she felt stronger each day. The nurses practically had to tie her to her bed to keep her in the hospital once she started feeling better. As soon as she could walk on her own, they sent her home. This was her first day back with the team.

"I'm gone for a few days and you guys stop taking your training seriously!" Megan chided the others. "Who put the UFO into the training program?"

The three drivers climbed from their simulator pods, removed their VR helmets, and headed to the control room.

"I didn't put that thing in there," Charger said.

"Don't look at me!" Stunts added, pretending to be hurt by the accusation.

"No way," Flyer added. "Not me!"

"Then who did it?" Megan demanded, tapping commands into the simulator's keyboard.

Charger looked around the simulator room and spotted his little brother, hiding, crouched behind a simulator pod. "Miles!" he yelled.

Miles sheepishly joined the group. "I was using the simulator to play Space Wizards," he admitted. "Guess I forgot to delete all the files. Oops! Sorry!"

"Well that explains that," Jack chimed in, giving

Miles a stern look, then spinning the boy's baseball cap around playfully. "Training's over for today. We'll need to debug the system before your next session."

Charger put his arm around Megan's shoulder. "It's good to have you back, Megan," he said, "I missed you." He quickly cleared his throat and added, "I mean, the *team* missed you. I mean . . . you know." Charger looked around, embarrassed, then turned and walked away, shaking his head. The other drivers followed him from the room.

Megan eyes tracked Charger as he left. She smiled. Her father stepped up next to her.

"I'll debug the computer, Megan," he said. "You need to rest."

"I've been stuck in that hospital bed 'resting' ever since the wreck!" she complained. "What I need is something to do so I don't go out of my mind!"

Jack smiled. "All right, *Spitfire*," he said, turning to leave. "Just don't overdo it."

Megan was finally alone in the room. She grabbed a VR helmet and climbed into a simulator pod. "I won't *over*do it," she muttered, grimacing with pain as she moved. "I'll just plain *do* it." Squeezing into the tiny simulator cockpit was never easy, but bruised as she was from head to toe, it was almost torture. Taking a virtual spin around the track wasn't the same as driving a real car, but at least the

simulator gave Megan a chance to get back into action without risking any further injury.

Settling into the driver's seat, wincing with the stiffness and pain, she pulled on her VR helmet and pressed the starter button in the cockpit.

"Okay, computer, give me a field of four cars," she ordered, "maximum difficulty."

11

*T*he image of *Big River Raceway* sprang up all around Megan. The computer didn't waste any time—it thrust her into the middle of a high-speed race.

Steering, shifting, and braking at the simulated 300-mile-an-hour-plus speeds all gave Megan pain somewhere in her still-healing body. She grunted and strained, and put the pain out of her mind. At least virtually, she was back behind the wheel of a NASCAR super racer, and there was nowhere in the world she'd rather be.

Upshifting and easing her foot onto the accelerator, Megan ripped past two driverless VR cars. Then a handsome human driver pulled his racer beside her. He smiled and waved.

"Good to see you back behind the wheel, Megan!" he called out in an easy, friendly voice.

"Hey thanks!" Megan replied without thinking. Then the fact that there was another human driver in her simulation struck her like an out-of-control supercar. *"WHAT?!"* she yelped, turning to the driver.

He quickly hit his rocket boosters and zoomed up the track away from her.

Megan slammed on her brakes and skidded to a stop.

She pulled off her VR helmet. Big River Raceway disappeared. She looked around at the other simulator cockpits. They were empty. "Miles!" she screamed. "Are you messing with the simulator again?"

There was only silence. "It can't be Miles," she realized. "There's nobody here but me. But then, who was I talking to?"

The climb out of the cockpit pod was just as difficult and painful as the one into it. Megan struggled to the ground and walked to the simulator control console.

"Computer, identify the driver in the car that passed me," she ordered.

"There is no other driver programmed in the race," the computer replied in a tinny, artificial voice.

"Well, he got in there somehow," Megan said, starting the painful climb back into the simulator pod. "And I'm going to find out how!"

Back in the simulation, Megan's car sped down the Big River Raceway track. "Come on, show yourself," she mumbled. "Whoever you are!"

Megan picked up speed, easily passing one driverless car after another.

Then she spotted him.

"I've got you now," she cried, stomping down on the accelerator and taking off like a shot.

Megan pulled alongside the driver.

He turned and gave her a thumbs-up signal. "Nice driving, Megan," he complimented her.

"Pull over!" she demanded. "Stop!"

But the driver picked up speed and pulled away. Megan upshifted and gunned her racer. She caught up to him easily.

"Who are you?" she asked, the annoyance showing in her voice. "And how did you get into the simulator?"

"Maybe I'm the man of your dreams," the driver replied, smiling. Then he sped up and started to pull away.

"In *your* dreams, maybe, fella," Megan snapped back, matching his speed and staying right at his side. "You've obviously accessed the simulator somehow, so just tell me why."

"Why?" the driver asked, grinning an even bigger

Team Fastex rides hard and fast to win the race for injured driver Megan Fassler, but Team Rexcor has other plans....

"All drivers to their cars!"

grin. "Because you're lonely and you need someone to talk to."

"I . . . I . . ." Megan stammered, confused by his answer. "You don't even know me!"

Megan felt a hand grab her shoulder. *"Yaa!"* she shouted in fright. Turning her head, she saw a floating hand—just a hand, no arm, no body—resting on her shoulder.

In the simulator room, Charger shook Megan's shoulder. "Are you all right, Megan?" he asked urgently.

Megan pulled her VR helmet off and the simulated world vanished, leaving the real world in its place. "Charger, you startled me," she shouted, annoyed at the interruption. "I was right in the middle of something!"

"You really think you should be using a simulator so soon?" Charger asked, concern showing in his voice.

Megan winced as she once again climbed down from the cockpit. "I'm just testing the debugging," she explained, as she walked to the control console.

"Those simulator pods are kind of rough on you," Charger said. "They bang you around just like the real thing."

Megan turned to face him. "I know!" she yelled. "I built the simulator!"

Charger stared at her a moment, then sighed and turned to leave.

61

"I'm sorry, Charger," Megan called after him. "It's just—"

"You're right," Charger cut her off. "It's your call, anyway." Then he left Megan alone.

She picked up the VR helmet and stared at it for a few seconds. Then she put it down and walked slowly from the simulation room.

That night, the Team Fastex garage was humming with activity. Air-powered wrenches whirred, hand tools clanged against engine parts, and feet shuffled along the cement floor.

Megan and Duck Dunaka were bent over an engine, half hidden under the hood of a Team Fastex racer, each wielding a tool.

"We'll have to make the final adjustments in the pit garage, right before the race," Megan announced.

Duck nodded in agreement.

"I don't want you in the pit tomorrow, Megan," Jack, who was keeping an eye on the pre-race preparations, told his daughter. "You're supposed to be resting, remember? Resting, not tearing down engines."

Megan pulled the upper half of her body out from under the hood. "I'm going to be driving again by the next race," she said defiantly.

"You have to get well first," Jack said with finality,

taking the air-powered wrench from her hands. "Now go to bed, and rest!"

Jack leaned over the engine, wrench in hand, and started to work with Duck.

Megan sighed and left the garage. She may have stopped working on the engine, but she had no intention of going to bed. "How can I rest," she asked herself, "when I don't know who or what this driver guy is?" She headed back to the simulator room.

Once again within the virtual world of Big River Raceway, Megan sat in her car, unmoving, staring at the empty track.

"Looks like I won't find this guy tonight," she said, sighing with disappointment as she reached to take off her VR helmet. "I guess I'm virtually alone."

Vrooom! VROOOOM!

The sound started softly, way off in the distance, then grew louder and louder as the racer approached.

"He's here!" she cried out with excitement. "I knew he'd come."

The mysterious human driver blew past Megan's car, followed closely by three evil-looking racers. These driverless cars were jet-black with brilliant red stripes on either side of their empty cockpits.

Megan started her engine, hit the accelerator, and zoomed onto the track in hot pursuit.

Two of the evil-looking cars pulled up on either side of the mysterious driver, slamming into him, while the third bashed him from behind. His rear bumper crumpled off and went flying past Megan's windshield.

"Hey! Watch it!" she shouted. "It's time for you to take a hike!"

Megan flipped the lever, igniting her rear jet boosters. Her car rushed forward from the force of the flaming jet engine. She powered hard into the back of the trailing racer, shoving it right off the track.

The black-and-red car careened into a VR refreshment stand, tearing it to bits, then dissolved into static and disappeared from the simulation.

"One down, two to go," Megan counted as she saw the two remaining driverless cars slow down, falling behind the mystery driver, moving right in front of Megan.

"Oh, no, you don't!" Megan cried.

She hit the jump lever on her dashboard, and wings popped from the sides of her car. Her boosters fired, and the car rose into the air, soaring over the red-striped racers.

The sinister racers both fired grappling hooks intended for Megan. Instead, the two hooks met, just below Megan's flying car, tangling together.

Thooom!

Megan's car dropped back onto the track in front

of the others. She slammed on her emergency brake, driving an anchor into the track. Her car stopped instantly. The black-and-red cars passed her on the left and right, still attached to each other by their tangled grappling hooks. The tangle of cables caught onto Megan's rear bumper—the one attached to the firmly planted anchor.

The grappling cables drew taut, and the two cars attached to them slammed into each other, exploding in an orange fireball, then disappearing from the simulation as well.

The mysterious driver pulled up beside Megan. "Great driving, Megan!" he called out to her. "Thanks for the help."

"Why were those cars chasing you like that?" Megan asked.

The driver glanced in his rearview mirror. "Looks like you'll get a chance to ask them yourself," he said.

Megan turned around and saw the same three black-and-red racers, obviously recreated by the simulation, tearing up the track, gaining on them.

Megan yanked her steering wheel hard to the right. "Follow me," she said, heading for an exit sign in the track wall.

The mysterious driver followed Megan past the sign, out of Big River Raceway, and onto the surface of Io—one of the moons of Jupiter!

The two NASCAR racers sat silently on the icy,

crater-filled surface of Io. Jupiter hung huge in the starry sky above them.

"Where are we?" the driver asked. "How did we get here?"

"I transferred us into a background file from a game that was on the simulator," Megan explained. The cars rolled forward, bouncing slowly along the moon's craggy, icy surface. "I don't think they can follow us here."

The mysterious driver looked at Megan. "You're pretty smart," he said, smiling. "And pretty."

Megan stopped her car and looked at the driver. "Okay, I've had enough of this," she said tersely. "Who are you, and how did you get into the simulator?"

The driver kept smiling. "Nothing's real in here, right?" the driver asked. "So let's play a game. I'll make you a deal. Help me win a race in here, and I'll tell you who I am."

Megan climbed out of her car and stood on the gleaming surface of Io. The mystery driver got out of his car as well.

"I don't make deals with people I don't know," Megan said. Then she stared intently at the driver for a few seconds. "I don't know you, do I?" she asked. "There's something familiar about you."

"Help me beat this simulator, and then you'll know everything," the driver replied evenly.

Megan kept staring at him. "Maybe you're not

real. Maybe I'm just hallucinating, an aftereffect of my concussion."

"If you are making me up, it must be because you need me as much as I need you," the driver offered. "No one should be alone."

Tears filled Megan's eyes, surprising her. The truth of the stranger's words touched her in a way she didn't expect. "I am alone," she said, reaching out to touch the mystery man's hands.

As their fingers touched, the driver dissolved to static and vanished, leaving Megan alone on the cold, alien landscape.

She pulled off her VR helmet and the background disappeared, giving way to the harsh light of the simulator room. Her tears, all too real, remained. "If only he *could* be real," she said softly to herself.

At that same moment, in the simulator room at Rexcor headquarters, the background of Io faded as the mysterious driver removed his VR helmet. As the scene changed to the reality of the Rexcor simulator room, so, too, did the driver's face change—to that of Lyle Owens.

"I've got to get me one of these," Lyle said to his fellow Rexcor drivers, putting the helmet down and climbing from his simulator's cockpit.

Specter, Junker, and Zorina climbed down from their simulator pods as well.

"Where did you two go?" Specter asked. He and his Rexcor teammates had been controlling the black-and-red racers that appeared to be attacking Owens in his disguise as Megan's mystery driver.

Spex rolled into the simulator room. "Mr. Rexton is here," he announced. Garner Rexton's face flared onto Spex's midsection video monitor.

"Did she fall for your line, Mr. Owens?" Rexton asked. "Will she help you win the race?"

"How could she refuse?" Owens answered. "I'm the man of her dreams."

Zorina rolled her eyes and whirled to face Owens. "And I'm your worst nightmare," she snarled. "Next time—"

Rexton cut her off. "Next time," he began, "she'll be racing against her own Fastex teammates. That's the whole point of this little ruse."

The three Rexcor drivers stared blankly at the image of Rexton.

"Allow me to explain," Rexton continued. "Megan knows everything about the Fastex drivers. She knows their strategy, their moves, their favorite tricks on the track. She knows how they will try to beat The Collector."

Owens smiled at the mention of his nickname.

"Only it won't be Lyle Owens they're racing against," Rexton explained. "It will be Megan. You see, Megan is going help us beat Team Fastex!"

12

*I*t was a beautiful morning and Big River Raceway was packed with eager fans anticipating the start of another Unlimited Division contest.

In the pit garage, crews hoisted cars onto hydraulic lifts, whipped lug nuts off tires, and in the case of Team Fastex, secured a section of fender into place with a freshly ripped piece of duct tape.

Up in Jack Fassler's office, in Team Fastex headquarters, Jack was finishing up a phone call. Megan paced impatiently in front of his desk.

"I'm on my way down right now," Jack said into the phone, then hung up. He turned to his daughter.

"Now what were you saying about the simulator?" he asked.

"I'm not really sure how to explain it." Megan's forehead wrinkled with concern. "All I know is when I was in the simulator—"

"You weren't suppose to *be* in the simulator," Jack interrupted. "You were supposed to be *resting*." He glanced impatiently at his watch. "Look, I have to head to the pit. We'll talk about this after the race."

Jack hurried from his desk and pulled open the door of his office. Charger was standing there, fist poised in the air, about to knock.

"What are *you* doing here?" Jack demanded. "It's almost race time."

"I just thought I'd see how Megan was feeling," Charger explained.

"She's fine," Jack answered curtly. "Now come on. *Let's get charged!*" Jack teased, tossing Charger's favorite psyche-up phrase at him.

Jack moved past Charger, who looked at Megan for a moment before turning to follow his boss.

Megan settled into the cockpit of her simulator. She pulled on her VR helmet and was instantly transported to the virtual version of Big River Raceway. "Where are you?" she asked, looking around at the empty track.

At that moment, at the real Big River Raceway, in the Rexcor hauler, Spex typed information into the hauler's communications panel. Next to the part-human, part-robot Rexcor crew chief stood Garner Rexton and Lyle Owens, who was already suited up for the race.

"Patch the controls of Owens car into the Fastex simulator," Rexton ordered Spex. "Then Megan will be driving her VR car—*and* your real car—against her own teammates."

Although Owens had agreed to carry out Rexton's plan, he didn't like the insulting tone of Rexton's voice. "Even if she does know how the Fastex guys drive," he barked at his boss, "I'm still a better driver than she is."

"Perhaps," Rexton replied. "Her own teammates might well beat her—if they knew *she* was driving. But they will think they are racing against *you* and use the wrong strategy!"

Spex handed Owens a helmet. "You will need this special VR helmet," he said.

"The moves that the Fastex drivers make against you won't work against her," Rexton continued. "The Fastex drivers will be confused and frustrated."

"And collected, by The Collector!" Owens added. At that, his frown changed to a smile, and he slipped the helmet on.

In her virtual simulation, Megan heard the sound

of an approaching racer. Her heart skipped a beat as the mystery driver pulled up next to her. "You'll have to get in my car," he explained.

"Your car?" Megan asked. "Why?"

"I want us to win this race together," the driver replied.

Megan shook her head. "That's not the way the simulator's programmed," she told the driver. "You can't have two people—"

Megan was cut off by a crackle of static. The image before her broke up into a million tiny computer pixels. Then it reformed—with Megan behind the wheel of the mystery driver's car, and him sitting beside her.

"—in one car," she finished, puzzled.

"This is *my* game, Megan," the handsome driver said. "I make the rules."

Megan looked around the track. Not only had she been transported to the mystery driver's car, but she now saw that the car was lined up at the starting line, with a full field of Unlimited Division racers on either side of her.

In the real Big River Raceway, the same number of cars were lined up at the starting line. The race Megan was about to run inside the simulator would match the real one at the raceway. The moves she made in Owens's virtual car in the simulator would also be made by Owens's real car on the track. However, on the real track, The Collector's car, con-

72

trolled by Megan, would be racing against Team Fastex!

"Drivers, start your engines!" the track announcer's voice boomed out over the public address system.

Engines roared to life all around The Collector. He made no move to press the starter button, but his own racer roared to life. "Hey, it works!" he said, thrilled that Megan's action—starting the "mystery driver's" virtual engine—had the same effect on his car in the real world.

Beside him in the simulation, Megan replied. "It does work, doesn't it?" she said. "I didn't know if I'd be able to operate your virtual car."

The cars in both worlds began to move, taking a warm-up lap. "It's kind of nice having a copilot," she added, smiling.

In the virtual world, Megan spotted a car up ahead rising up onto two wheels, showing off for the appreciative crowd.

"That's funny," she said, puzzled. "That's just like the move Stunts does."

In the real world, Stunts had indeed gone up onto two wheels. Owens, alone in his real car, watched his steering wheel, gear shift, and gas pedal all move seemingly by themselves, responding to Megan's moves in the simulator. *I could get used to this*, he thought.

The huge electronic flag over the starting line turned green—the signal to start the race.

Engines screamed to life as the racers of NASCAR's Unlimited Division blasted off into another high-speed battle.

Around and around the track they zoomed, bunched together like a darting, weaving school of fish. Every time one driver seem to be pulling ahead, someone else took the lead. Precious little daylight could be seen between the cars in this bumper-to-bumper speedfest.

In the simulation, Megan faced the same pack of tightly bunched racers. She turned her wheel left, then right, jockeying for an opening.

"These cars are programmed better than anything I've ever driven against," she told the mystery driver in the seat next to her.

"You can beat them," he replied confidently. "If you really want me to tell you who I am."

A VR racer pulled up right on Megan's tail. The car moved low on the track, then swept high, trying to pass her.

"If you can make the rules, so can I," she said. Megan sharply pulled her car up the track, cutting off the passing VR racer. Its left front wheel bounced off her back fender, sending the VR car spinning wildly into the track wall.

At the real Big River Raceway, Charger's car, which had attempted to pass Owens, spun out of control and bounced off the wall as well. Charger

stumbled to a shuddering, smoky stop, then he restarted his engine and headed for the pit.

In her simulated racer, Megan looked puzzled. *I know I've seen that move before*, she thought. She shrugged and went after the car in front of her.

Charger pulled into the Fastex IMP. Duck was in the mechanic's seat running the pit stop. Mechanical arms sprang to life, changing tires, refueling, and checking out the damage from the impact of the crash.

"What's going on out there?" Duck asked Charger through the racer's window. "It's like The Collector knows everything you're doing before you do it."

"It's not just that, Duck," Charger explained. "He's got all different moves, like it's not even him driving!"

13

*O*ut on the track, *Stunts pulled up*
behind Owens and Junker, preparing to pop up
onto two wheels and slip between them—his signa-
ture move. "I got you guys right where I want you!"
Stunts said with a grin.

In the simulation, Megan spotted a virtual car in
her rearview mirror in exactly the same position as
Stunts in the real race.

"He's setting up for a pass," she said. "Almost
exactly the way Stunts would. But I'm not going to
let him!"

Megan swiftly downshifted and tapped her brakes. This slowed her car enough to get in the way of the virtual car behind her, which had just started to rise up onto two wheels. Megan bashed into the VR car, tipping it over—and taking the real Stunts with it.

"He saw me coming!" Stunts cried, as he pulled the lever releasing his Rescue Racer. "Owens knew I was going to make that move and reacted much faster than I've ever seen him react." Stunts's Rescue Racer sprang from his car, soared into the air, and landed right on top of Specter's racer.

"No hitching, Stunts!" Specter cried. Then he stomped on his brakes, squealing to a stop. Stunts's Rescue Racer flew off his roof.

Whomp!

The Rescue Racer landed hard, banging down onto the track. "Omph!" grunted Stunts, jolted and shaken as Impact Foam—a safety foam released to cushion a driver from the impact of a crash—filled the inside of his Rescue Racer. Stunts slowed and headed for the pit.

In the simulation, Megan's car sped along the virtual raceway. The disguised VR image of Owens, which sat next to Megan, cried out in joy. "We're gonna take all of them!" he shouted.

"It's easy to win when you don't have to drive by the rules," Megan pointed out. But her voice was puzzled. "What I don't understand is where the

computer learned those tricks it's making the other cars do? It's as if I'm racing against Team Fastex."

Owens shrugged. "Maybe the simulator's programming the VR cars to drive like Team Fastex," he suggested.

"Yes," Megan said, although she didn't really sound convinced. "That must be it."

The remaining racers roared around the track at Big River Raceway, still bunched close together. The Collector and Zorina held a slight lead, giving Team Rexcor a momentary grasp on first and second places. But Flyer and Charger were right behind them, quickly closing the gap.

Flyer lined up directly behind Charger. "Ready for the slingshot, Charger?" he called to his teammate over their helmet radios.

Charger reached for the lever that fired his booster rockets. "Then let's get charged!" he shouted. Charger fired his rockets and prepared to pass Owens on the low side of the track.

In her VR car, Megan anticipated the move. "If those were Fastex drivers," she said, "they'd try to pass low."

"Here they come!" the mystery driver shouted in the seat next to her.

"Hang on!" she called.

Megan downshifted and spun her wheel hard.

78

Her car fishtailed wildly, violently waggling across the track—just as, on the real track, Charger made his move to pass Owens!

"What's The Collector up to now?" Charger wondered, watching the back of Owens's car swing back and forth.

Slamm!!

The back of Owens's shimmying racer bashed into Charger's front end, sending him veering sideways down the track. Charger crashed through an infield barrier and slid out of the race.

"All right!" the mystery driver cried in the seat next to Megan. "One more for the collection!"

Megan's skin went cold. Now she understood. "The collection?" she whispered.

The handsome mystery driver squirmed in his seat next to her. "I—I mean the collection crew," he stammered, desperately trying to cover his slipup. "You know, the crew that cleans up after the race."

Megan looked right at the no-longer-quite-so-mysterious driver next to her. "*You're* The Collector," she said quietly, lips tight, eyes narrowing.

"I don't know what you're talking about," Owens lied.

"It's you, Lyle!" Megan shouted, getting angrier by the second. "This is all some kind of Rexcor dirty trick! And I fell for it . . . like a fool!"

"Come on, Megan," The Collector pleaded. "I thought we really connected."

"Well, this connection is terminated!" she yelled back.

Megan cranked hard on the steering wheel.

Bammm!

She slammed hard right into the VR car to her right. On the real track, Owens's car rammed into Zorina's.

In the simulation, Owens reached over and tried to grab the wheel from Megan. "What are you trying to do?" he demanded.

"Stop you from winning!" she snapped back, shoving his hands away.

On the real course, Zorina was furious. "Knock it off, Owens!" she screamed, slamming her car into his.

"It's not me!" he shouted back, bouncing around inside his racer. "It's Megan."

Megan continued to ram her car into the VR car next to her, certain it was having the same effect on Zorina in the real world. "You wanted me to drive!" she snarled at Owens. "Well, I'm driving!"

Zorina watched and laughed as Owens's car slid toward a ramp in the raceway infield. "Bad luck, baby!" she cackled, momentarily distracted by the sight. But in the high-speed world of NASCAR Unlimited Division racers, a moment is all it takes to bring disaster. Zorina looked back in time to see her car drive straight into the track's wall.

She opened her mouth to scream. "Grumpt!

Mrrmpt!" was all that came out, as her car—and her mouth—filled with Impact Foam.

In the simulator, Megan floored the accelerator.

On the real track, Owens screamed "Nooo!" as his car rocketed up the ramp, soaring wildly into the air.

In the Rexcor hauler communications room, Spex spoke to Garner Rexton over his video monitor. "We have trouble," the robotic crew chief told his boss.

"This isn't trouble!" Rexton raged. "This is total, undeniable failure!"

Owens's car continued its airborne journey. It sliced right through the Rexcor hauler's communications tower. The tower fell to earth with an ear-splitting *blaaammm!!*

Owens's racer finally splashed down, like some demented space capsule, in the middle of the infield lake. The Collector scrambled from the sinking wreck just before it disappeared below the water's surface.

14

Junker and *Flyer* roared into the final stretch, with Junker in the lead. Flyer moved high on the track and began to pass.

"Junk is not winning races!" Junker screamed.

Junker slammed his car into Flyer's, sending it lunging toward the wall.

Flyer fired his wings and booster rockets, taking to the air just as Junker tried to slam him. With Flyer's car off the track, Junker hauled hard on his steering wheel and bashed his own car into the wall, taking himself out of the race.

Flyer retracted his wings and returned to the track, just in time to cross the finish line!

Megan sat in the virtual wreckage of her car, which rested in a crater on the moon, Io. A distorted image of Jupiter hung eerily in the night sky. Next to Megan sat the image of Lyle Owens.

"Now that I know who you are," she said sadly, "you even look like The Collector."

Then Owens's face morphed from that of the handsome mystery driver into his own. "You know, it's true what I told you, about you needing me," Owens said. "You're lonely, and you always will be."

Megan stared at Owens. "I'm reprogramming the simulator so you can never hack in again," she said coldly. "So stay out of my reality, Owens!"

At that The Collector dissolved into static.

Megan removed her VR helmet. The background of Io disappeared. Megan climbed from her cockpit and strode through the empty simulator room.

Alone.

Charger rushed in, barely able to contain his excitement. "Megan!" he called. "I didn't know if you knew. We won the race. Flyer won!"

Megan smiled. "I know," she said. "I almost feel as if I had been there."

15

*O*n a night when he should have slept soundly—the night of his victory at Big River Raceway—Flyer struggled with a nightmare. Instead of dreaming about the glorious events of that day, he suffered through his darkest moment, reliving it in his sleep, as he had done so many times before.

In the nightmare, Flyer was once again an Air Force fighter pilot, on a dangerous top secret night mission. He was wearing his Air Force uniform, complete with helmet and night-vision goggles. His plane flew low over an endless stretch of desert.

"Target acquired," Flyer announced from the cockpit of his fighter jet. "Let's put these bad boys out of business!"

Flyer's thumb flipped the protective cover off his missile launch button—then fired.

Missiles streaked from beneath his wings and swiftly found their target—a low, sprawling military complex that would have blended into the desert even in the daytime.

Fwwoooooommm!

The missiles rained their fiery destruction down on the complex, lighting up the night sky. Orange flames and black smoke rose from the mangled building.

And over that, a cloud of red chemical smoke rose from the ruins.

At that moment, two soldiers on the ground fired shoulder-launched surface-to-air missiles that tore into the night sky. One of the missiles exploded right next to Flyer's fighter, sending him tumbling out of control.

"I'm hit!" Flyer shouted into his radio, struggling with the plane's controls, trying to guide his fighter out of its end-over-end somersault.

The red chemical cloud reached him. The sickly red mist splattered against Flyer's windshield, blocking his view, then seeped through a crack in the glass and filled the cockpit. Flyer's eyes burned,

his lungs fought for air, and his fighter jet raged out of control!

"Nooo!" Flyer screamed—

—and woke up. Gasping for breath and covered in sweat, Flyer sat straight up in a chair in the driver's lounge at Team Fastex headquarters.

He held his right hand out in front of his face. It trembled. He grasped it with his left hand and forced it to stop. Flyer sucked air into his nostrils. Slowly, his breathing returned to normal, though his mind raced with worry.

Flyer heard the lounge door open, then footsteps. He rearranged himself in the chair and tried to look as if everything was normal as Megan walked into the room. *Ha! Normal,* he thought. *That's a joke.*

"Are you okay, Sharp?" Megan asked, using Flyer's real name.

Flyer spun his chair so that his back faced Megan, giving himself a few more seconds to recover from the nightmare and the shaking. "Yeah," he replied. "These chairs aren't as comfortable as they look. I must have dozed off. Woke up in a funny position." He stood and crossed to his locker. "I'm going to head home. What about you?"

Megan grabbed a clipboard and moved for the door. She was still sore, but felt noticeably better with each passing day. "Duck and I still haven't tested all of the new off-road equipment we've added to the cars. So, I'm off."

She reached the door, then turned back to her teammate.

"Oh, again, great race, Flyer," she said. "You really saved it for us . . . for me, after that VR trick I fell for. Thanks!"

"What?" Flyer responded, still distracted. "Oh, hey, that's what being teammates is all about."

Megan nodded, then headed back to the garage.

Flyer looked at his hands again. They shook uncontrollably.

Out at Big River Raceway, the lights normally used for night racing illuminated the track and the makeshift dirt practice strip Duck had set up in the infield.

Stunts sat behind the wheel of his car on the dirt strip. Duck and Megan had equipped the racer with a few special off-road accessories.

"Now take it slow till you get the feel of it," Duck instructed Stunts.

Stunts grinned broadly. "Slow and careful, Duck," he said. "Like I always do."

Almost before he had finished the sentence, Stunts hit the accelerator. His tires squealed against the dirt as he peeled out, sending a shower of dust over Duck.

Stunts roared down the dirt strip, building speed. Then he jerked the wheel hard to the right, pur-

posely sending himself into a skid. His car lost traction on the slippery sand and slid sideways.

"Time to put on my dancing shoes," Stunts said as he flipped a newly installed switch on his dashboard labeled TRACTION TIRES.

Instantly, curved spikes snapped out of the tire treads, digging into the dirt. Just as fast, the car stopped skidding and straightened out—heading right for the asphalt track.

Stunts pulled hard on the wheel, trying for a tight U-turn, which he made. Unfortunately his car spun into the "U" on the asphalt, its traction spikes still extended.

The sharp metal claws tore chunks of asphalt from the beautiful, smooth raceway. Black divots flew into the air, leaving gaping holes in the sleek surface.

"Retract!" Duck yelled into his radio. "Retract the spikes!"

Stunts hit the TRACTION TIRES switch and the gleaming claws pulled back up into the tire treads—just as Stunts returned to the dirt strip!

The spikeless tires spun the car out of control. Stunts flipped end over end, bouncing and rattling in the cockpit, which filled with Impact Foam. The racer finally came to rest nose-down in the dirt, rear end sticking straight up into the air.

"Carlos!" Megan cried out in concern. "Are you all right?"

Megan and Duck rushed to the flipped-over car, just in time to see Stunts wriggle through the window, spitting out Impact Foam.

"Phoo-y," Stunts spat a glob of foam onto the ground. "Off-road racing!" he growled. "NASCAR drivers are meant to race on asphalt!" Then he stormed off to get cleaned up.

Duck looked at Megan. *"He's* all right," Duck said, pulling a roll of duct tape from his tool belt and heading to the damaged car, which was another story.

16

*B*right moonlight lit up the Team Fastex headquarters parking lot. But Flyer could have easily found his SUV without the extra illumination. He was the last one out of the building, which meant that his was the only vehicle parked in the lot. Or so he thought.

He had paced the floors of the driver's lounge until his hands stopped shaking and his mind calmed a bit, but only a bit. Then he dressed in his street clothes—a long-sleeved shirt open at the neck with its sleeves rolled up two turns, comfortable jeans, and his favorite cowboy boots—and marched purposefully to the parking lot.

He started his SUV, whipped it into reverse, and glancing over his shoulder, backed up.

An ominous-looking black sedan pulled right into his path. Two burly men in military uniforms leaped from the car.

Flyer threw the SUV into first gear and eased up the clutch. He rolled forward only inches before a second, identical sedan pulled in front of him, completely blocking the SUV.

Furious, Flyer switched off his engine and flung open his door.

"Hey!" he shouted. "Move it or lose it!"

A thick, leathery hand caught the door, stopping it cold. Glaring down at Flyer was the unmistakable, deadly serious face of a military intelligence officer.

Flyer had met more than his share of these types—single-minded, humorless tough guys—during his time in the Air Force. The uniform was a dead giveaway, but Flyer could pick out one of these guys in a clown costume. The face alone—weathered, chiseled, clean shaven, with piercing, know-it-all eyes—told him everything he needed to know.

The officer leaned down, his bulky body blocking the door, making it clear that Flyer was not going anywhere.

"I'm Colonel Straub," the officer said. "We need to talk, Captain Sharp." It was an order, not a request.

91

Flyer looked wary. "I'm not a captain anymore," he replied. "I'm a driver. I resigned from the Air Force." Then he slammed his door shut and restarted his engine.

Colonel Straub leaned in the window. "Did you also resign from your country?" he demanded. "You don't have to wear a uniform to serve."

Flyer ignored him, jockeying the SUV back and forth until he had just enough room to slip by the sedans. He put it in gear and started to drive off.

"I'm talking about saving lives, Sharp!" Straub shouted at the retreating vehicle.

Flyer slammed on his brakes and stuck his head out the window, looking back at Colonel Straub.

"You're the only man who can carry out this mission," the colonel said firmly.

Flyer looked at the colonel, then at his hands, which still gripped the steering wheel. They were rock steady. Not that fear would have stopped him. If Flyer was the only man who could accomplish a mission to save lives, there was *nothing* that would stop him. He opened the door and stepped from the SUV. "What kind of mission?" he asked.

"Top secret," the colonel replied.

Flyer's body tensed. He knew all too well what those words meant.

"Top secret," the colonel repeated. "You understand me, Captain? Even your own teammates can't know about it."

Flyer's posture straightened, his face revealing no emotion. He was suddenly, once again a soldier following orders. "Understood, Colonel," he replied.

Colonel Straub's black sedan cruised along the main highway leading through New Motor City. The impressive skyline was lit up against the black sky. Flyer had forgotten just how beautiful the city looked at night. He stared out the window and took a deep breath, then focused his attention on Colonel Straub, who was seated next to him in the backseat.

"His name is Brock Vanleer," Straub began, holding out a photo for Flyer to see. "Former U.S. Army. Major. Chemical warfare specialist. Disappeared three years ago. We believe he's set up his own chemical weapons facility. You know, sell to the highest bidder, terrorists, whoever has the cash."

Flyer nodded.

"We think his factory is in Secado," Straub went on.

"Secado?" Flyer asked, surprised. "That's where our next race is. Out in the desert."

"We think his base may be only a few miles from the racecourse," Straub pointed out. "But before we can mount a full strike, we need to know exactly where he is. That's where you come in."

Straub reached into his briefcase and pulled out a small black box with several dials and an LED readout. Two antennalike probes extended from the top

93

of the box. Straub handed the box to Flyer. "And, that's where this little device comes in," Straub explained. "It can detect trace elements in the air of the chemicals he's using."

Flyer looked the device over as the black sedan pulled back into the Team Fastex headquarters parking lot. He got out on one side of the car as Straub stepped out the other.

"What if I'm captured by Vanleer?" Flyer asked, heading for his SUV. "If he finds this thing in my car—"

"He won't search your car," Straub interrupted. "Why should he, when he *knows* you're not an agent?"

Flyer looked puzzled. "How would this wacko know anything about me?" he wondered.

"Didn't I tell you?" Straub asked, smiling for the first time. "He's a big racing fan!"

17

*T*he blazing midday sun beat down in the cloudless desert sky. Waves of blistering heat rippled off the vast expanse of endless sand. The wind was still, but a dust cloud rose and rushed across the landscape like a giant sandstorm.

Vroooommmm!

Team Fastex blasted across the desert, practicing for their first off-road challenge.

Sand blew into Charger's open window. "Hey, Stunts!" he squawked over the car's radio. "What does the name of this place mean in Spanish?"

Stunts's car was also swirling with sand. "Secado?" he replied. "It means 'dry,' amigo!"

"Well, they got that right!" Charger shot back.

Stunts fired his maneuvering jets, lifting his racer up onto two wheels.

"This is just a practice run, Stunts," Megan said, activating her radio-transmitter. "Save the showing off for the race, will ya?" Megan could hardly keep the smile out of her voice—she was thrilled to be back behind the wheel of a real racer. The doctors had cleared her for racing that morning. Equally important, her father allowed her to rejoin the team. No more simulations. This was the real thing.

Stunts tore through the sand on two wheels. "I'm practicing showing off!" he cried.

"Come on, guys," Megan pleaded over her radio. "No more fooling around!"

Stunts dropped back onto all four wheels and the team slid down a steep ledge, into a gully, driving in tight formation.

"Let's keep this as close as we can to actual race conditions," Megan requested.

"Maybe we can help with that," a staticky voice crackled over all four Team Fastex radios. It was a familiar enough voice—Lyle Owens!

The Collector tore up the road in his Unlimited Division racer, flew off the lip of the gully, soared over all four Fastex cars and landed in the sand just in front them.

"Rexcor!" Megan shouted, catching sight of Owens.

At that moment each of the other three Rexcor drivers launched their racers off the gully's lip.

Zorina's car splashed into the sand, only inches from Flyer. He swerved, narrowly missing her.

Junker's car slammed down right in front of Charger, just as Specter's car clipped Charger on the side fender. Both Rexcor drivers accelerated, pulling away and spraying Charger with a wave of sand.

"That does it!" Charger shouted into his radio. "It's time to kick some serious bumper!"

Charger and Stunts upshifted, gunned their engines, and started gaining on the Rexcor four.

Megan, meanwhile, looked around for Flyer, who had slowed down and dropped back.

"Everything okay, Flyer?" she asked.

"It's my engine," Flyer reported over his radio. He had never been a good liar, and lying to a teammate like Megan was very tough. "It's, um, it's running hot," he stammered uncomfortably. "I—I'm going to have to drop out."

"Okay, Flyer," Megan replied. "We'll see you back at the pit." Then she zoomed off in pursuit of the others.

When Megan had disappeared into the sandy horizon, Flyer stopped his car and pulled out the chemical measuring device Colonel Straub had

97

given him. He activated the device, which gave out a steady beep. "A negative reading," he muttered to himself, checking out the device's meter.

Looking out over the expansive desert, Flyer saw the dust trail of the racers in the distance, veering to the left. To the right, an old dirt road led up into the mountains. He put his car in gear and headed to the right.

The perfect silence of the desert was shattered by the roar of seven NASCAR Unlimited Division racers. A lizard, out sunning itself on a rock, skittered into a crevice as the roar passed by.

Megan, Stunts, and Charger pulled up on the Rexcor drivers, who still held the lead. Charger moved to pass Owens, who swerved to block him.

Specter and Junker, racing side by side, separated a bit. Stunts saw his opening. Thrusting up onto two wheels he slid into the narrow space between the Rexcor racers.

Which is exactly what they were counting on!

Junker and Specter waited until Stunts was directly between them, then they slammed back together, bashing into Stunts from both sides.

Stunts grunted from the jolt of the impact and struggled to keep his car balanced on two wheels. He was pinned between the two Rexcor racers, with

no room to bring his car back down onto all four tires.

"Hang on, Stunts!" Megan called. She fired her booster rockets and jumped right over The Collector— only to have Zorina angle right into the spot where she was headed. Megan cut her rockets and dropped down behind Zorina to avoid another catastrophe.

Zorina bashed her as she landed.

"Not again!" Megan spat through gritted teeth. "I will not go down again!" Then she sped up, close on Zorina's rear bumper.

Meanwhile, Junker and Specter sandwiched Stunts again, trying to knock him over. Again Stunts maneuvered to keep his balance on two wheels.

Junker grinned at Stunts, who grinned back and pointed to the other side of Junker's car. Junker turned his head and spotted Charger, now racing beside him, smiling and waving.

"I am very much not to like this!" Junker shouted.

Charger and Stunts returned the favor, slamming into Junker from either side, sending him spinning wildly.

"Consider yourself junked!" Charger cried.

Junker's car spun right toward Megan. She swerved, but not quite in time.

Whooom!

Junker's spinning wreck caught Megan's right fender.

99

"Umph!" she cried, rocked from the jolt, trying to right her car, spinning dizzily in the sand. *Stay with it*, she said to herself. *You won't get injured again!*

Megan wrestled the wheel under control and twirled to a stop, many yards off the course. She tried to back up, but her wheels just dug deeper into the desert sand. She shifted forward. Same result.

Charger and Stunts both slammed on their brakes and whipped around throwing up a shower of sand, heading back to see if Megan was okay. They were far more concerned with their teammate's well-being than they were with beating Rexcor in a meaningless practice run. Especially after all that Megan had just been through.

Amazingly, Junker kicked his engine back on, and roared back onto the course following his teammates, despite the damage to his racer.

Megan stepped from her car. She was fine. Her car, though, was stuck in the sand.

Charger and Stunts pulled up beside her. "Let's get you out of here!" Charger said, when he saw that she was all right.

Megan got back into her car and fired her boosters. The left side of the car popped off the ground, just as Charger's grappling hook grabbed it and yanked it forward. Megan's tires spun until finally they got traction, and her car lurched forward, free of the sand, stopping only inches from where Stunts stood.

100

"Wouldn't it have been easier just to have Duck send out an IMP?" Stunts asked.

Charger cocked an eyebrow. "You want to tell him the day before a big race that we banged up our cars playing tag with Rexcor?"

"Good point," Stunts admitted.

Megan leaned out her window. "I can't raise Flyer on the radio," she reported. "We'd better backtrack and see if we can pick up his trail."

Flyer's racer bounced along a dirt road through the craggy barren desert hills. The sun still bore down with blistering heat. The dust he kicked up made Flyer choke and cough. He slipped between two big boulders, jolted by deep ruts in the long-neglected road, and approached an abandoned-looking mining facility. The little black box Colonel Straub had given him beeped. Flyer stuck it out his window, and it beeped faster.

"Hmm, picking up something, finally," he said to himself.

At the same time as he was monitoring traces of chemicals in the air, Flyer himself was being monitored. The camouflaged gun barrel of a hidden tank now swiveled and lined up Flyer's car directly in its sights.

A tall man dressed in safari clothes crouched nearby, radioing instructions to the tank's comman-

der and to his boss. "Crane to base," the man said into a handheld radio-transmitter. "We've got an intruder."

"We're on it," came a voice crackling through the transmitter's tiny speaker. "We'll take care of him in the usual way."

"Understood," Crane replied. "Fire the tank!"

18

"**H**old your fire!" Crane's radio crackled. The tank commander heard the order as well.

In an office deep within the not-so-abandoned mining facility, the man behind that voice sat at a dusty old desk staring at a portable video monitor. On the monitor, Flyer's car moved slowly up the dirt road toward the facility. Speaking into a handheld radio-transmitter identical to Crane's, the man at the desk couldn't hide his surprise or his excitement. "I *know* that car," he explained to Crane.

Flyer's racer approached the mining facility. He

drove slowly past an empty, run-down hangar, several jeeps covered by camouflage netting, and a ramshackle mining office.

The closer he got, the faster the measuring device beeped. He switched off the chirping black box and spoke into a radio transmitter on his dashboard.

"Sharp to Straub," he said. "I'm getting a strong reading on trace chemicals." He flipped the switch down, waiting for a response, but heard only static. "I can't get a message through these mountains," he groaned to himself. "I'd better look around first, anyway."

Flyer stepped from his car and strode over to the mining office. As he reached for the door, it was pulled open from the inside. The man who had been sitting at the dusty desk stood before him. Flyer recognized the man from the picture Straub had shown him. It was Brock Vanleer!

"I didn't think there was anybody here," Flyer said, a bit startled.

"The mine's closed down," Vanleer explained. "I'm an engineer. I'm checking to see if it's worth reopening."

Flyer felt uncomfortable. "I, uh, I was wondering if I could get directions," he lied. "I'm a driver with the Unlimited—"

"I know who you are," Vanleer interrupted. "And I know why you're here."

Flyer froze in terror, unsure what his next move should be.

Vanleer slipped a hand inside his jacket.

Flyer's whole body tensed. Was Vanleer going for a gun?

Vanleer pulled out his hand. In it he clutched an official NASCAR Unlimited Division season guide. "Any chance you could autograph this for me, Flyer?" he asked, holding out a pen, as well.

Flyer breathed a sigh of relief and happily signed the guide.

"I recognized your car from a picture in the racing guide," Vanleer explained. "That's quite a set of wheels you've got."

"I got separated from my team during a practice run," Flyer said, handing the guide and pen back to Vanleer. "In fact, I'd better be getting back. If I backtrack on this old road, will it take me to—?"

Flyer was interrupted by the sudden appearance of Crane, the sentry who had first spotted him.

Crane stepped up behind Flyer. "You can't leave now," he said.

Again Flyer tensed up, preparing himself for a fight.

"You can't go before we get a picture with you, right?" Vanleer asked. "I'll get my camera."

Vanleer stepped back into the office and snatched his camera off a shelf. His videoscreen beeped, then filled with the image of Garner Rexton.

"Where have you been, Vanleer?' Rexton demanded.

"We had a little emergency, Mr. Rexton," Vanleer replied.

Rexton's expression turned sour. "Not too busy to talk with the man who is bankrolling your entire operation, are you?" Rexton asked sarcastically.

Vanleer stared at the videoscreen nervously.

"I have an overseas buyer with an urgent need to oppress his neighbors," Rexton continued. "How much chemical agent can you ship by tomorrow?"

Vanleer thought for a moment. "Thirty drums, by oh-six-hundred hours," he replied.

"That will have to do," Rexton said. "Now, what was your emergency?"

"We had an intruder," Vanleer explained. "But it's just a Team Fastex driver who got lost."

Rexton's face grew huge, filling the videoscreen as if it was going to burst right through and into the office. "What!" he shouted.

Vanleer was puzzled by his boss's furious reaction. "They're doing a practice run near here," Vanleer said. "For the Desert Five Hundred."

Rexton's face hardened into a cruel mask. "Kill him," he ordered calmly.

"He's just a driver, Mr. Rexton," Vanleer said, shocked by this request. "He doesn't know anything about our operation here."

"Fastex is the enemy," Rexton lectured. "When an enemy is in your power, you destroy him!"

Rexton's face vanished from the videoscreen, replaced by the crackle of blue static.

Vanleer methodically put down his camera, opened the center drawer of his desk, and pulled out a gun.

"Well," he said, sighing deeply. "At least I got his autograph first."

19

Flyer stood halfway between the mining office and his racer. Crane stood behind him.

Vanleer emerged from the office and leveled his gun at Flyer.

"That's not a camera," Flyer said, his mind racing, trying to buy some time and figure a way out of this situation, which had just become a major problem.

Vanleer looked away. "Well, actually," he began, a little embarrassed by what he was being forced to do. "We're not mining engineers." He really would have preferred to have simply taken a picture with Flyer. He was, after all, a big fan. But business was business, and when you worked for Garner Rexton, sometimes that business got nasty. Very nasty.

Flyer shrugged and lifted his hands, palms up. Then he swiftly reached back and grabbed Crane's arm. Dropping into a crouch, he flipped the larger man over his shoulder, right onto Vanleer.

Flyer bolted for his car. He had to get in, get the engine started and get out of there before Vanleer recovered.

Or so he thought.

Flyer skidded to sudden stop when he reached his car. In a flash he was surrounded by a dozen men— hired guns, mercenaries—all aiming automatic weapons at him.

"Hold your fire!" Vanleer ordered, as he stepped up behind Flyer. "Throw him down the mine shaft. No one will find his body there." Vanleer started to walk away. Then he stopped and added, "unless Flyer really *can* fly."

Vanleer and a few of his men led Flyer at gunpoint into the huge run-down hangar next to the office. The building may have looked a wreck, but the operation inside was sophisticated and high-tech all the way. Enormous enclosed vats filled with toxic chemicals were tended by teams of technicians.

Giant mixing blades stirred the vats, combining the chemicals into just the right deadly formulas. Across the hangar, a small twin-engine cargo plane sat beside a pile of metal drums. The drums, filled with finished chemicals, were being loaded onto the plane for shipment.

Flyer spotted a clear vat filled with a bubbling red liquid. He paused, staring at the churning mixture. His thoughts flashed back to his nightmare and the horrifying red mist that haunted his dreams.

"That red chemical," he asked, pointing at the clear vat. "What is it?"

Crane shoved him forward.

"It's not deadly, if that's what you're worried about," Vanleer replied. "It's a 'fear agent.' It gives its victims a chemically induced panic attack. Sweating, increased heart rate—"

"Trembling hands," Flyer finished. His mind raced. *Could this be the reason for my panic attacks?* he wondered. *Could it be this simple?*

"I forgot," Vanleer said, breaking Flyer from his own agitated thoughts. "The racing guide said that you were in the Air Force. You ever run across this stuff?"

Flyer looked down at his hands, then back at the vat of bubbling red. "I don't know," he replied. He saw himself once again in the cockpit of his fighter, the red cloud slamming into his wind-

shield, seeping into the plane, stinging his eyes, burning his lungs. . . .

"Keep moving!" Crane said gruffly, shoving Flyer again, snapping him back to his not-too-promising present.

Vanleer jogged across the hangar to talk with the men loading the metal drums into the plane.

Flyer stopped short and spun toward him. "Vanleer!" he shouted, his voice echoing across the open hangar. "Is there an antidote?"

"We've got the antidote right here," Vanleer called back, slapping his hand down onto a bright yellow metal drum. "Hey! You mind if I take your car for a spin later?" Vanleer laughed at his little joke and turned back to business.

Two of his hired hands shoved Flyer to the edge of a deep mining shaft. His feet stopped short at the edge, knocking a few pebbles into the opening. The tiny stones fell for a long time before they finally hit bottom. It was a long, long way down.

The portable radio on Vanleer's belt squawked. "Outpost Seventeen to base," said a scratchy voice. "Three unauthorized vehicles have crossed the perimeter. They look like three more racers."

Vanleer frowned. "Must be visiting day," he said into the radio. "Destroy them!"

Flyer pulled his elbow straight back into Crane's gut as he kicked out, knocking one of Vanleer's

111

thugs into a stack of barrels. The barrels cascaded across the hangar floor. Flyer was fighting not just for his own life, but for the lives of his teammates as well. Lucky for them all, Flyer had special Air Force training in hand-to-hand combat.

Another mercenary lunged at Flyer, who side-stepped. The man stumbled and fell into the shaft. Then Flyer made a run for the hangar door.

Crane raised his gun and trained it on Flyer's back.

"Hold your fire!" Vanleer ordered. "One spark and this whole place could go up in flames!"

Crane grunted, then holstered his firearm and dashed after Flyer, followed by three more mercenaries.

Flyer lowered his shoulder and took out three startled technicians like a running back slamming into a linebacker. He barged through the hangar door—which slammed right into another hired gun. The mercenary's partner raised his weapon, but Flyer brought the palm of his right hand up into the man's chin, knocking him backward.

Crane and the mercenaries stepped from the hangar and opened fire.

Automatic weapon fire sprayed all around him as Flyer leaped into his car, punched the starter, and roared down the dirt road.

Vanleer screamed into his radio. "Code one secu-

rity alert!" he bellowed. "All units stop that driver! Now!"

Mercenaries whipped the netted camouflaging off their motorpool, then spilled into their jeeps and the humvee, tearing down the road after Flyer.

Two helicopters took to the air, roaring past the hangar, closing in on the supercar.

At the base of the hills, Megan, Stunts, and Charger powered up the dirt road. The hidden tank rotated its big gun and caught the three driver in its sights. The tank operator had his orders. He was about to fire.

Flyer skidded alongside the tank, tossing up a huge arc of sand, blinding the tank commander just as he fired . . . and missed his target. The ground near the three drivers exploded in a shower of sand.

"What was that?" Charger shouted into his radio.

The two choppers roared overhead, unleashing a strafing run of bullets at the four Fastex cars.

"What is going on here?" Stunts shouted.

Megan roared toward a sand dune. A huge jeep carrying four mercenaries flew over the dune— right at Megan!

She swerved to avoid the jeep and narrowly missed slamming into Flyer, who spun to a stop next to her.

"Flyer!" she yelled into her radio. "Who are these guys?"

Stunts whipped his wheel back and forth, trying to stay away from the strafing chopper fire. "We figured you'd busted a radiator," he said. "Not started a war!"

"I don't think we can outrun those choppers!" Flyer announced to his teammates. "We'll have to take 'em out!" Flyer came about and headed toward one of the choppers.

"Flyer!" Megan yelled. "What are you doing?"

Flyer yanked the grappling hook lever on his dashboard. "A little fly-fishing," he growled.

The grappling hook fired from the back of Flyer's racer, snagging on the landing gear of the first chopper. "I caught me a whopper!" Flyer shouted, as he whipped his car into gear and tore across the desert at high speed.

The slack in the grappling hook's cable disappeared. Powered by the mighty Unlimited Division engine in his racer, Flyer towed the chopper behind him. The copter's pilot fired wildly, spraying bullets randomly across the sand.

Flyer shifted into high gear and drove right through a low stone arch—not too low for his racer, but much too low for the chopper, which rammed into the structure, exploding in a massive fireball.

Shock waves rippled through the desert from the impact of the explosion. In the cockpit of his racer, Charger winced from the intensity of the shaking

and the sound. "This is crazy!" he shouted to the others. "We're not soldiers!"

Thoooomm!

A shell from the second chopper exploded next to Charger's car, flipping it up onto two wheels. Charger struggled to hang on, riding a thin line of balance until his airborne wheels returned to the sand.

"Hey!" he shouted angrily. "We're not pushovers, either!" He spun in a circle and roared up an embankment toward the second chopper.

Fooosh!

Charger's car flew off the embankment, catching air, then catching the chopper's spinning rotor right in its windshield. The rotor made its final swipe right through the car's cockpit. Charger ducked to avoid getting beheaded by the flat sharp blade, then plunged into the sand, tearing the rotor completely from the chopper.

Charger's car filled with Impact Foam. He scrambled out just in time to see the chopper crash a short distance away. "That was a close shave," he said, wiping some foam from his cheek.

The chopper crew staggered from their wounded bird, shaken and stunned. They dropped to the sand and covered their heads as the chopper blew, sending a plume of red flames and black smoke skyward.

Stunts plowed through the sand, roaring past a

steep hill. The tank appeared from nowhere, flopping down over the crest of the hill, landing inches from the front of his car. He turned and braked to avoid getting crushed by the tank's devastating, relentless treads.

"Stunts!" Megan called into her radio. "Get out of there!"

Before her teammate could respond, Megan's rear window shattered in a hail of bullets.

20

*A humvee burst through a billow-*ing smoke cloud, bearing down on Megan, machine guns spitting hot metal.

Megan glanced back over her shoulder. The humvee looked as wide as the desert itself as she swerved left, then right, to stay clear of the raining lead.

Stunts saw Megan in trouble. He swung around and behind the humvee. Flooring his racer in a burst of speed, he wedged his hood under the humvee's high rear axle.

"I want to teach you guys my favorite trick,"

Stunts said to the angry mercenaries shaking their fists at him from the back of the humvee.

He fired his left side maneuvering jets, lifting his car—and the humvee—up onto two wheels. Stunts jerked his wheel to the right, then quickly back to the left, tossing the humvee off his hood, flipping it over onto its roof.

Still on two wheels, Stunts skimmed past a jeep. The jeep's driver panicked and peeled off into a ditch. Stunts dropped back down onto all four wheels and raised his fist in triumph.

"You guys are good," he said. "But you're not NASCAR material!" Then he sped ahead and caught up with Megan.

Flyer circled the tank. With each pass, the gun turret swiveled in vain, trying to catch up with Flyer's streaking racer. Each shell it fired exploded just behind the car.

"Hang on, buddy!" Stunts shouted as he joined Flyer. "It's time to double-team this tin can!" Stunts fired his boosters and leaped into the air, slamming down right on the barrel of the tank's gun. The massive weight of his Unlimited Division car bent the tank barrel, pointing it right at the ground. The gun then fired, blowing a huge crater in the desert.

Megan raced alongside the tank, her tires tossing clouds of sand onto it.

Blinded by the sand, the tank driver steered the

mammoth rolling weapon right into the crater. It rolled helplessly over onto its side, landing with a sickening crunch.

Flyer, Stunts, and Charger—whose car ran despite its run-in with the chopper—pulled up alongside Megan.

"Everybody okay?" Charger asked.

Megan shook her head in disbelief. "Dad's gonna have a cow," she moaned. "If he thinks racing against *cars* is dangerous . . ." She didn't have to finish the thought.

"Hey, that wasn't so bad," Stunts said, looking around at the wrecked humvee, jeeps, helicopters, and tank. "At least, now that it's all over."

"But it's not over!" Flyer cried. "Vanleer's still got the toxin." He jammed his car into gear and streaked back up the dirt road toward the mine, leaving his teammates in his sandy wake.

Back inside the hangar, Vanleer shouted into his radio. "You're telling me that they destroyed both choppers, the tank, and all the jeeps!" he shrieked at the mercenary on the other end.

"And the humvee, sir," squawked a voice from the handheld unit.

"Noooo!" Vanleer screamed, flinging the radio away. It smashed into a metal drum and shattered.

"Rexton will have my head for this." He turned to the few remaining mercenaries. "Get the plane ready for take-off," he barked. "We're getting out of here!"

The huge hangar doors swung open as the twin engines of the small plane roared to life.

At the same time, Flyer reached the mining complex and skated toward the hangar, heading straight for the plane.

Vanleer picked up the deep distinctive roar of Flyer's engine above the high-pitched whine of the idling plane. He grabbed a missile launcher from a startled mercenary, aimed, and fired right at Flyer.

The missile sped from the hangar out toward Flyer. It exploded right beneath his car, sending the super racer hurtling out of control.

Flyer weaved into the hangar, bashing through vats of toxic chemicals before scraping to a screeching stop.

Vanleer leaped into the plane, which taxied toward the open hangar doors.

Flyer and his car leaned over onto one side. He held his hands out. They were shaking. His windshield was coated with dripping chemicals. "I can't let him get away!" he snarled. Then he fired up his turbojet boosters. Searing flames poured from the back of his racer, igniting the chemicals.

The fire spread quickly among all the toxins. The hangar was soon engulfed in flames. A wall of fire flared up, blocking the hangar door.

120

The small plane dashed right at the raging flames blocking its path. The pilot shot a panicked look at Vanleer.

"Keep going!" Vanleer ordered threateningly.

The pilot picked up speed and the plane knifed right through the wall of flames, still heading for the hangar door.

That's when Flyer spotted a barrel of the antidote, just twenty feet away across the burning building. He looked from the antidote back toward the plane, then back at the barrel again. There wasn't time to get to the antidote *and* stop Vanleer. Flyer had to make a choice.

"No," Flyer said to himself. "I have to stop him." He fired his maneuvering jets and popped the car back onto its wheels. Then he sped off, tires squealing, racing after the escaping plane.

The plane burst from the burning hangar with Flyer gaining on it. The small plane was no match for the speed of a NASCAR racer on the ground. Flyer was only inches away from the plane's tail when it lifted off.

Inside his car, Flyer's face dripped with sweat. His hands shook as he struggled to maintain his grasp on the steering wheel. "I can do it," he spat out between tightly clenched teeth.

Flyer popped his wings out and kicked in his rear rocket boosters. He shot into the air, just high enough to ram the tail section of the rising plane.

Flyer's racer returned to the ground—followed closely by the plane's tail section, and then the rest of the plane.

The damaged plane turned in an out-of-control arc and plummeted back toward the flaming hangar.

"No!" shouted Vanleer.

Garner Rexton sat in his massive office watching a wall-size video monitor. He stared at the empty mine office, his rage building. "Vanleer!" he shouted at the huge screen. "Where in blazes are you?"

Rexton caught sight of the burning hangar, then saw the plane taxiing wildly toward it.

"Nooo!" whispered Rexton.

Then the giant screen went blank.

Whhhooooommm!

Vanleer's plane hit the hangar and exploded, launching Vanleer and the pilot into the air. They landed on the ground with a thud.

Vanleer lurched to his feet, then stumbled into a cloud of red mist that was pouring from the hangar. His lungs burned and his eyes stung. His hacking, choking cough could be heard across the compound. Then he disappeared into the billowing plumes of red smoke.

122

Flyer sped from the smoldering ruins of the mining facility, still trembling, still sweating.

His heart pounded like a hammer in his chest as he rejoined the others at the bottom of the mountain.

Megan, Stunts, and Charger leaped from their cars and rushed to Flyer.

"Sharp!" Megan cried. "Are you okay?"

Flyer climbed from his car, battered, bruised, and still shaking. He nodded at his friends.

"You sure, amigo?" Stunts asked. "You're shaking like a leaf!"

Flyer held his hands out in front of him. They trembled uncontrollably.

"It'll stop," he said, looking back at the red smoke drifting over the horizon. "Maybe someday." He sighed deeply. "For now, though, I'm glad to still be alive," he said, mustering up a smile. He glanced around at his brave and loyal teammates—Charger, Spitfire, and Stunts. Flyer had never been so happy to see a group of people in his life. "Thanks for helping me take out those goons."

"Hey!" Stunts replied with his trademark grin. "What are friends for?"